PENGUIN BOOKS
GOING TOO FAR

Caroline Lassalle was born in London. Educated at Oxford, she married and went to South Africa, where she lived in various places and did various jobs. Gradually becoming involved in anti-apartheid activities, she was eventually arrested and held for five months in solitary confinement without any charge being brought against her. Released, she returned to England, where she became founding editor of Picador Books. Under a pseudonym she has written four thrillers that she describes as 'very black comedies'. Her first novel, *Breaking the Rules* (1986), is also published by Penguin. Caroline Lassalle has one daughter. She lives in Cyprus with her second husband, the author George Lassalle.

CAROLINE LASSALLE

GOING TOO FAR

PENGUIN BOOKS

PENGUIN BOOKS

Published by the Penguin Group
Penguin Books Ltd, 27 Wrights Lane, London W8 5TZ, England
Penguin Books USA Inc., 375 Hudson Street, New York, New York 10014, USA
Penguin Books Australia Ltd, Ringwood, Victoria, Australia
Penguin Books Canada Ltd, 10 Alcorn Avenue, Toronto, Ontario, Canada M4V 3B2
Penguin Books (NZ) Ltd, 182–190 Wairau Road, Auckland 10, New Zealand

Penguin Books Ltd, Registered Offices: Harmondsworth, Middlesex, England

First published by Victor Gollancz 1989
Published in Penguin Books 1991
1 3 5 7 9 10 8 6 4 2

ACKNOWLEDGEMENTS

Fond thanks to R.A., E. de K., S.F. and R.H. for information; to A.C. for salvage;
and to M.D.: polymath, polyhistor

The quotation on page 36 is from "Return of the Golden Age" by Mazisi Kunene
in *Ancestors of the Sacred Mountain*, published by William Heinemann Ltd
and reproduced by kind permission of the author.
The quotation on page 71 from "Spain 1937" by W.H. Auden,
taken from *The English Auden* edited by Edward Mendelson,
is reprinted by permission of Faber and Faber Ltd.
The poem on page 162 is "The Poet" from *Sonnets to Orpheus* by Rainer Maria Rilke,
translated by Selden Rodman in *100 Modern Poems*, published by New American Library Inc.
Part title decorations are by Andrew Fowler

Printed in England by Clays Ltd, St Ives plc

For George

CONTENTS

MORNING

"Such a lot of stones," said Johnny Fairfield.

At the back rose the stony hillside, up which ran a narrow bleached path. In front lay the pebble beach. Out at sea were the three big rocks. (Sea-urchins clung to them, just as spiny plants like hedgehogs clung here and there to the stones on the hill.)

Delia Ellis said, "They're different from English stones. More like the stones back home."

"Always harking *back*, Delia." Johnny yawned.

"The Mediterranean is neutral," said Bettina Bernstein. "Separating Europe from Africa, and belonging to neither."

"Stones," Delia said. "Those yellow Cotswolds. Everyone told me they were lovely. I tried to like them, but it was no use. They were so bland. Bland and cold, like frozen custard."

"Tourist traps," said Johnny. "Bolt-holes for ghastly Birmingham businessmen."

Delia said, "You're as snobbish as ever. Not that I have any time for *businessmen*, but——"

"Shakespeare's countryside," said Bettina.

Bettina's house—whitewashed, roofed with terracotta tiles—was between the hillside and the beach. Two-thirds of the back of its large, paved terrace was covered by wooden slats. Over these spread a vine which, on each side, trailed to the ground, forming a leafy curtain. Between the slats hung heavy bunches of grapes: dark, swollen, and with a dusty bloom. A green-shaded lamp, its flex attached to one of the slats, was suspended directly above a pale, varnished wooden table. Four rush-seated chairs stood round this table. Behind it was the open front door.

On either side of the door was a window covered by a decorative wrought-iron guard, painted white. The grey shutters of both windows were fastened flat against the wall. Over the window beyond the vine-sheltered area —on the side of the terrace where steps led down to the beach—was a faded blue awning.

At the front of the terrace, under a hot sun, Johnny, Delia and Bettina faced the sea.

In navy-blue swimming-trunks with a designer's monogram, Johnny lay—arms tightly folded, legs crossed at the ankle—on a pink canvas stretcher. Over the back of it hung a light-blue towel. On a small table beside him were cigarettes, a battered metal lighter, an ashtray and a bottle of suntan oil. Under the table was a zipped black travelling-bag. Johnny wore sunglasses with very dark lenses. Under a coating of oil his skin was tawny. Straw-coloured, like his hair, his long moustache was a well-pruned growth of shrubbery in the tidy landscape of his face. As the top section of his stretcher was up-tilted, he could study his handsome feet. Across the front of each, just below the toes was a tattoo: RIGHT on the left foot, LEFT on the right.

Delia glistened as if just painted with a rich orange-brown liqueur. Around her neck—a thick column that merged into heavy shoulders—hung the long strands of her black hair. Wearing a dilapidated red bathing-dress, faded and a couple of sizes too small, she sprawled on a green cotton-covered mattress. A book, pamphlets, writing-equipment, packets of chewing-gum and a roll of peppermints spilled around her from a frayed raffia basket. Tanned, her flesh looked firm; in contrast to its darkness her teeth looked white. From her debris she emerged, a large bronze from a messy excavation.

Johnny on her right, Delia on her left, tall, skim-milky Bettina sat in a white basket chair. Her narrow, beautiful mouth was pink. Her dark-brown hair was parted in the middle and coiled in a skein on her nape. One pale thin hand with silvered nails rested on a round white table. A large umbrella, attached to the table, contained her in blue shadow, and she wore a blue kaftan. Bluest were her eyes, large and clear under painted eyebrows, curved and black. On her feet were thonged sandals, and an ivory crab hung from her neck on a silver chain.

"This weather's sensational." Johnny lit a cigarette with his battered lighter. "I'd never have believed it could still be so hot in late October."

"But Bettina says they need rain badly." Delia shifted and frowned.

Bettina said, "Yes, the rain's late this year."

Johnny laughed. "It can rain as much as it likes when I'm back in London."

"Irresponsible as ever," said Delia. "Anyway, when will *that* be? You've stayed here six weeks already, haven't you?"

Bettina said, "And he's still not as brown as you are after two days."

"I never turn that colour," said Johnny. "My mother would say that you must have a touch of the tar-brush, Delia."

"It's a shitty expression. But I wish it was true. No evidence, though." Delia blew out her lips like a horse.

"Phew, I'm thirsty. Since I gave up the booze I'm always thirsty." She laughed loudly. "Think I'll go and get a soda water."

Bettina said, "Wouldn't you rather have some Perrier? There's plenty."

"No thanks. Ordinary soda's fine. Shit! Can't really tell the difference. No need to waste your posh, pricey mineral water on me." Delia prepared to heave herself up.

Bettina looked at her small flat watch. "Don't disturb yourself. It's eleven. We might as well bring out the drinks trolley."

"My appointed task!" Johnny sprang, boyish, to his feet. Stretching, he looked out to sea. "Those three rocks looming there," he said. "Like Gorgons."

Bettina said, "Gorgons aren't made of stone. They turn people into it."

"My mistake."

"They have yellow wings and brazen hands and bodies covered with impenetrable scales. Two are immortal, but the third—Medusa—wasn't. She was very beautiful. She had snakes instead of hair."

"Sounds perfectly disgusting," said Johnny.

"When Perseus killed her, he flew off with her severed head. The drops of blood that fell from it became the snakes of Africa."

"Ugh," said Johnny.

"Poor Africa," said Delia.

"Darling Bettina, how learned you are." Johnny was still looking out to sea. "Perhaps," he said, "I don't mean the Gorgons. Perhaps I mean the Furies."

"Really? The three Erinyes? They're snake-haired, too —but *far* worse than the Gorgons. A burning torch in one

14

hand, a whip of scorpions in the other. Black and bloody garments—"

"*Très chic*," said Johnny.

"They're attended by terror, paleness and death. On earth they exercise vengeance through wars and plagues; in hell through constant torture and continual flagellation."

"Awfully kinky!"

Bettina said, "But they also have another name. The Eumenides. The Kindly Ones. Perhaps they were first called that when they stopped pursuing Orestes for the murder of his mother. Perhaps the name was meant simply to flatter and soothe them. Or it could be just a euphemism." She paused. "People are always afraid of giving dreadful things their real names."

Johnny said, "The Kindly Ones, indeed! A likely story!"

"In any case, I don't think you're talking about *them*, either. *I* think you're talking about the three Fates. There's Clotho—she holds a distaff and controls the moment of birth. Lachesis carries spindles; she spins out deeds and events. Atropos—she's the eldest—wears a black veil, and holds a pair of shears to cut the thread."

"The thread?" said Johnny.

"The thread of life." Bettina paused. "Atropos is inexorable. They all are. Even the gods can't overrule them."

"And they're women," Delia said with satisfaction. "Gorgons, Furies, Fates—all women!" She added, "And all threes."

Johnny said, "I'm meant to have had a classical education—"

"At that English, so-called—ha ha!—*public* school of yours," interposed Delia.

He ignored her. "But I can't remember any of this stuff. It was all soldiers and senators. I shall fetch the drinks." He crossed the terrace, was dappled by the vine, disappeared into the long dim hall beyond the door.

"Then there were those three goddesses," Delia said. "Juno, Minerva and Venus. The Judgement of Paris. Venus won, didn't she? Paris gave her an apple and she gave him Helen of Troy."

Bettina said, "I always prefer to use the Greek names. Hera, Athene, Aphrodite. I feel that the Romans polluted everything they inherited from the Greeks."

"Oh really? How?"

"They were such go-getters. Empire-builders. Vulgarians."

"Shit! They sound just like Americans," said Delia. Then, "I remember I always thought Juno—Hera—was boring. A bossy housewife."

Bettina said, "But very powerful."

"I would have chosen Athene."

"I can understand why. Wisdom. But war as well. And what about her perpetual virginity? No, it must be Aphrodite for me. Anyway there's something unique about her."

"Paris obviously thought so."

"Oh, that was just a beauty contest. I mean something different. I think of her as *in the beginning*. Emerging from the sea."

"It sounds Darwinian."

"Yes, in a way."

Glass shimmied as Johnny came out of the house, trundling the drinks trolley, and halted in the shade of the vine. At the sight of the trolley's load—garnet, amber and diamond liquids, struck by points of light pricking between the leaves; an enormous white ice-bucket and big silver tongs; two vociferously yellow lemons—Delia's expression brightened, then, instantly, dimmed.

"You said just soda, Delia?"

"Afraid so." The loud laugh.

With the tongs Johnny dropped an ice-cube into a squat, dimpled tumbler. He poured soda on top, then carried the drink to Delia.

"Thanks," she said, taking a gulp as soon as the glass was in her hand.

"Bettina?" said Johnny.

"Oh. Campari-soda, please."

He chose a fragile tube in which he built a pyramid of ice-cubes. He added a thin slice of lemon and a squeeze of oily juice from the zest. He measured out the red aperitif, then carefully poured on the soda. Lightly, with a long spoon, he stirred the mixture.

"There we are," he said, putting the glass on the table beside Bettina.

She studied the rise of rosy bubbles. *Pretty!* she said. "Thank you, Johnny. And what about you?"

"Bloody Mary. But I'll have a quick swim first."

Bettina briefly closed her eyes against the glare. She said, "I don't know how you can, in this blazing sun."

He said, "Ice maiden!"

"Maiden?" She smiled.

"Snow Queen, perhaps."

Delia said, "I feel too lazy to swim." She had finished her soda water, and was leaning on one elbow. Now she picked up a book that was lying, face down, beside her.

"This book!" She held it up so that Bettina could see the dust-jacket, which showed a Palladian house in line and wash; blurred, or perhaps rain was falling. "It's shitty."

"Is it?" Bettina took a first sip of her drink. "I ought to have read it. The author sent it to me."

"Yeah. He's written inside it. 'To La Belle Bettina.' And the hero's called Piers. I ask you!"

"Is he a peer, this Piers?" asked Johnny.

"No, but his dad is. *He*'s called Peregrine. Shit!"

'So Piers is a peer's heir. Awfully suitable." Johnny crossed the terrace, pausing by the stretcher to pick up his towel and his black zipped bag. Carrying them, he went down the steps leading to the beach.

"Why does he take that bag around with him everywhere?" said Delia.

"Can't imagine. Just one of his idiosyncrasies."

"I once saw a play where the murderer carried a head around in a bag."

Bettina said, "Johnny's bag's too small."

Delia laughed. Then she said, "*I* always like to swim directly after lunch."

"My mother said it was bad for one."

"So did my dad. He was the one that laid down the law. Yuck! And it's such nonsense. A lovely big meal, a bottle of wine. . . .' She paused, then said, "Whoosh!" With her left arm she made a plunging movement in the air.

Bettina sipped again, then put down her glass. Beside it on the table was a clean white ashtray in which lay a packet of Disque Bleu cigarettes and a small silver lighter. Now she took a cigarette from the packet, and lit it.

"Your second today?" asked Delia.

"Mmm."

"Five a day! Shit! If I could do that, I never would have given up.'

Bettina said, "It's a matter of discipline."

"For me, it's all or nothing." Delia made an obliterating gesture. "I kept getting bronchitis. It was interfering with my work. But I hate having given up. It's so bourgeois and cowardly to stop smoking." She laughed. "And almost as dreary as giving up drink."

Now she was watching Johnny, through the rail. "Those hot pebbles don't bother him at all," she said. "He's got tough South African feet like mine. Not like your sensitive English tootsies. I always think they're so sweet, those little blue shoes you wear in the sea. Look at the way he runs. Sort of in slow motion. He could be in a television commercial. For a deodorant, perhaps. Always so hot to seem cool, our Johnny! I don't trust him an inch. Do you?"

"Trust him?" said Bettina. "I never really think of him in those terms."

"But you *like* him? I mean, you see a helluva lot of him, don't you?"

"Yes, I do. In a way, he depends on me, I think. We're such old friends. And he can be such a charmer."

Delia said, "For me, friendship implies trust." After a moment she added, "I suppose he does have charm, but—shit!—he's so superficial. And those ridiculous tattoos on his feet that he had done when we were at varsity—you'd think he'd have had them removed by now."

"I believe it's very difficult and painful to remove tattoos."

"His hair has faded. So have his eyes. Of course, most of the time he keeps them hidden behind those sunglasses. I don't think he's nearly so good-looking as he used to be—though the moustache helps. Do you remember that time he shaved it off? He grew it again pretty quickly."

Bettina said, "I think he felt he looked vulnerable without it."

"A bit vacuous, *I* thought. And he's so twitchy nowadays. As if someone was pulling strings and pressing buttons behind his face."

Bettina said, "He has suffered."

"Suffered!"

"He had two very bad breakdowns."

"Breakdowns!"

"He tried to kill himself. Twice."

"Tried! Anyway I can't see any reason for him to do that sort of thing."

"You know, Delia, one doesn't have to be black or starving in order to suffer."

After a moment Delia said, "Why hasn't he got a job? Even one of those shitty jobs he used to go in for— advertising, public relations, all that crap—would be better than nothing."

"It's not easy nowadays. Especially when you're getting on for forty."

"Our Johnny! One of the unemployed! Lolling by the Mediterranean."

Bettina said, "He's having a bit of a rest at the moment. But he'll go back soon, when he feels up to it. He does look for jobs, you know. He quite often gets one. Keeping it's his problem."

Delia laughed.

Bettina said, "It's not funny, really. Things go wrong for him."

In the pause that followed, Delia unwrapped two

peppermints and put them in her mouth. Crunching, she said, "I remember, at varsity, everyone thought he was in love with you. He used to hang around—oh, so casually—whenever you were due for lectures."

Bettina smiled. She shook her head. "Those lectures! I was always taking a course in something. Psychology, History of Art, the Victorian novel. I liked to get out of the house." Again she closed her eyes against the glare. "Durban! The northern suburbs! White houses. Green lawns. Purple bougainvillaea. Turquoise swimming-pools."

"Black servants," said Delia.

"Yes, indeed . . . plenty of those."

Delia said, "I remember a party with food floating on fake water-lily leaves in the swimming-pool."

"Not one of *my* parties."

"Shit, no. . . . It was a lady called Sheila something."

"Sometimes I'm charmed by the sheer exuberance of really bad taste. Sheila Gordon?"

"Yeah, that's right. All those ladies were fascinated by people from varsity. By lecturers. Even by students. They thought we were *bohemian*. They used to take us to that Italian restaurant with the candles in bottles. I remember picking off the wax as it hardened. One of the husbands would pay the bill."

"Yes, Max often paid."

"Oh, I wasn't thinking of you and Max," Delia said quickly. Then, "There was a pianist."

"Yes. He used to play *La Mer* whenever I came in."

"Why *La Mer*?"

"I can't remember."

Delia said, "Johnny swims with his watch on."

"It's waterproof."

"Shit! It would be. I haven't been wearing my watch

here. It's so great to get away from time. Mario's—that's what it was called, that restaurant. Of course *you* were always quite different from the other northern suburbanites. I remember your tyres screeching as you turned into the car-park at Howard College in that little navy-blue Karmann Ghia of yours, with its open top, and your hair blowing—you used to let it blow in those days." Delia put two more peppermints in her mouth. She said, "*I* never thought Johnny was in love with you. I thought he was fascinated by your being so beautiful and chic. And English. And rich. And older—"

"Only two years," said Bettina.

"It seemed more because you were married. Being married was part of your fascination too, of course. Our Johnny always liked other people's women. He used to go around with couples. Three was always company, for *him*. Of course, even then, I guessed what *that* implied."

"Here he comes."

"He never swims out to the rocks. Always out into nowhere and then back again. Mr Nobody, going nowhere."

"Delia, you're absurd."

"Mr Nobody," Delia repeated. "I think one day he'll vanish. Simply fade away and vanish. Or perhaps he'll leave a grin behind, like the Cheshire Cat in *Alice in Wonderland*. To show off those well-kept teeth."

Johnny was smiling as he came up the steps. He hung his towel over the terrace rail. "That Bloody Mary is calling me awfully loudly," he said. "Just a quick shower first, though." Carrying his black bag he crossed the terrace, and went into the house.

"Bag in hand," said Delia. "Like a commercial traveller with his samples." Then, "Just a quick swim, just a quick shower," she mimicked. "I can't think why some people always rush to shower when they come out of the sea. It's like washing right after one's washed."

"Not really," said Bettina. "I always have a bath after I've swum. The salt's so bad for one's skin."

"Oh, is *that* what Johnny's worried about?"

"I expect he likes to get rid of the sticky feeling."

"But it's so lovely."

"Does everyone have to like what you like, Dee-dee?"

"Nobody's called me that for years. I thought I couldn't stand it. But when *you* say it, I feel nostalgic."

She picked up the book with the line-and-wash dust-jacket, but read for only a few seconds. "Piers! Peregrine! Shit!" she exclaimed, and slapped the book back on to the mattress.

Bettina said, "You shouldn't leave books open and face down like that. It's bad for them."

"Oh, I'm sorry." Delia picked up the book, shut it, put it down again. Then she said, "Somehow, I've never really been interested in books, as *objects*. As *property*. Only in what's inside them."

Bettina's eyes were closed now. Delia took another two peppermints. There was only one left in the roll. After an instant's hesitation she added it to the two in her mouth. She screwed up the wrappings and dropped them onto the book beside her. She said, "People bath and shower too often nowadays. Especially white South Africans. It's neurotic."

Bettina smiled, but did not open her eyes. There was a silence.

Johnny came out of the house, carrying his bag. Now he was wearing light-blue trunks and a white T-shirt with *Ganglion* printed on it.

"*Ganglion*?" said Delia. "Why *ganglion*?"

"They're a group. Surely you've heard of them?"

"No. Should I have?"

"They're awfully well known. Anyway, I thought you kept in touch with these things. For *fund-raising*."

"Not with *Ganglion*. Do you think they'd be sympathetic?"

"To *the cause*? I haven't the faintest idea." He was standing by the drinks trolley. "Bettina?"

"Not yet." Her glass was almost full.

"Delia?"

"Yes, please."

With a tiny sigh he crossed to her. He stooped and picked up her glass. "Same old soda?"

"Yeah."

"I would have thought . . . when you're on holiday. . . ." he said.

She spoke brusquely: "Absolutely not." Then, "Shit. It's a pity my deadly sins are so unfashionable. Gluttony and sloth. I suppose drinking—and smoking, too—count as gluttony."

Bettina said, "Sloth? Gluttony? What are you talking about, Dee-dee? You work like a slave, and you've given up drinking and smoking."

"Not eating, though. Anyway the point is that it's all against nature. Every inch of the way. Do you remember Hans Andersen's Little Mermaid when she got feet, and every step she took felt as if she was walking on a sword? That's me—ha ha! Shit, what I'd really like to do is just lie in the sun, swigging and puffing and guzzling."

"Then why don't you?" said Johnny. "Especially during your holiday." He gave Delia her soda, and went back to the trolley.

She said, "It's quite fashionable to be lustful or avaricious. Nobody objects to *those* sins. People admire them."

Bettina said, "There's meant to be a new sexual puritanism in the air."

"Oh, AIDS and all that." Delia glanced at Johnny, busy concocting his Bloody Mary.

He looked up, and said, "Lust doesn't bother you, Delia? How surprising!"

"Why surprising? Of course, everyone's always thought I must be terribly sexy because I'm so dark and have a big bust. But on the whole I rather prefer a good dinner. Sad!"

"Oh, I don't know," said Bettina. "Good dinners are easier to find than good sex."

"But there's the guilt one feels after one's eaten them. All those calories. Whereas sex is more like slimming, really. The exercise, you know."

Johnny said, "Goodness, you must be awfully energetic. Anyway, good food doesn't have to be fattening." Bag hanging from his left hand, Bloody Mary in his right, he returned to his stretcher.

"Oh, shit! Don't tell me you really enjoy that *cuisine minceur*, or whatever it's called?"

Johnny said, "That's pronounced 'mahnseur', not 'minsewer'. Anyway, it's out of fashion. Nowadays the point is to eat *healthy* food."

"Healthy food! I don't believe there is such a thing. There's just nice food and nasty food. Besides, it's all so *boring*—this health business. And the people who go in for it are bores too. Just like religious fanatics. It was the priests who used to push us around. When we got rid of them, we might have had some fun, but now the doctors have put on the priestly robes."

Bettina said, "Now people believe in the body, but not in the soul."

"The body's all one's got, so one had better take care of it," said Johnny.

Delia said, "Shit! People used to abstain from things for moral reasons. Now they do it for health, so health has become moral. People are actually shocked when other people do unhealthy things. It's nauseating. Look at the way they bully smokers. And, do you know, I read an article by some ghastly woman the other day called, 'I'd rather be dead than fat'?"

Startled from her wrath by Bettina's and Johnny's simultaneous laughter, Delia frowned, smiled, then frowned again. "No, it's no joke. Rather be dead than be Balzac or Flaubert or George Eliot or Matthew Arnold?"

"*Matthew Arnold*?" said Johnny.

"Yeah. He weighed seventeen stone."

"I don't dispute it. But who was he? Just a boring old Victorian headmaster."

"That was his father. Matthew was a poet.

> *Down, down, down*
> *Down to the depths of the sea.'*

Johnny raised his eyebrows.

"Then there was Dr Johnson—not that I can stand the pious old bore, but I'd sooner be him than be some half-witted journalist. Shit!—rather be dead than be Stendhal or Henry James?"

"The heavy mob," murmured Johnny.

"It's symptomatic," Delia went on. "*They* only care about appearances. Simple-looking clothes that cost a fortune. Tiny helpings of incredibly expensive food. Perrier. That's really why I won't drink it—because *they* do."

"*They*?" asked Johnny.

"The cool ones. How I hate them. They have no passion."

"Coo-er," said Johnny in a cockney accent. "Oo'd a thought it? *Pashern*—well I never did!"

"No, Johnny, I'm quite sure you 'never did'. Because passion's not cool. It's *extreme*. Balzac was extreme—as well as being fat. When he was working, he ate nothing but boiled eggs, and drank cup after cup of black coffee."

"Cholesterol! Caffeine!" Johnny exclaimed.

"He used to get up in the middle of the night, to work. Then he would put on a pure white robe. He said that, to write, one should wear garments without spot or stain. He wrote with a quill from a raven's wing."

Bettina said, "I like that very much. I love it. The pure white robe and the raven's feather."

"Yeah, but when he wasn't working, he was quite different. At dinner someone once saw him eat a hundred oysters, twelve cutlets, a duck, two partridges, a sole, a dozen pears and a helluva lot of sweets. His table manners were lousy. He used to blow his nose in his serviette."

"Table napkin," said Johnny, and then, "ugh!"

Delia said, "I admire it all. I admire the recklessness. *They* would never be bad-mannered. *They* would certainly never eat too much. Elegant little shits! It might spoil their pretty figures."

Bettina said, "And yet you often go on diets, Dee-dee."

"Yeah." Delia's look was rueful. "It's against all my

principles. But people don't take you seriously, now-adays, if you put on too much weight. You make a bad impression at work."

A muscle twitched at the corner of Johnny's mouth, and he brushed his hand over it. He said, "So you diet for *the cause*? How awfully noble."

Bettina smoothed her smooth hair. "Dee-dee, just now, when you said that lust was smart, you said that avarice was, too. Darling, surely not?"

Johnny said, "But of course not. Nobody likes mean-ness. Everyone thinks it's squalid to be stingy."

"Is that so, Johnny? Is that so? Anyway, avarice doesn't mean stinginess. It means cupidity. Greed for money. Love of it. Money's OK nowadays. People don't despise it, or even pretend to, as they did in our day."

"Our day!" said Johnny. "Our sloppy, soppy, simple day!"

"You didn't feel like that about it then. You were too busy smoking *dagga* and taking weird pills and listening to deafening music. You were really part of the Swinging Sixties."

Johnny said, "How awfully scathing you sound. I thought you *liked* that time."

"I did. I do. But not that shitty stuff. It was the idealism that attracted me."

Johnny groaned. "*We shall overcome*. Overcome *what*?"

"I've heard that joke before. It was Martin Luther King who first said 'We shall overcome,' and he died for it. If you want to know what *I* want to overcome, I'll tell you. Racism. Capitalism. War-mongering. The beastly bourgeoisie that everyone aspires to belong to nowadays. They all sweat away, just to make money, and they're proud of doing it. They call themselves workaholics, and when they say it, they actually sound *proud*."

Johnny said, "You do surprise me, Delia. I thought you approved of work. 'The dignity of labour.' 'Workers with hand and brain.' I'm sure I've heard you use those very clichés—sorry, I mean phrases."

"Oh, I believe in work that has a real purpose. Of course I do. But not in working just to make a lot of shitty money. As you said about Balzac—*ugh*!"

Johnny said, "Your kingdom is obviously not of this world, Delia. Holy poverty and Martin Luther King. Have you taken to religion?"

"Oh, of course not. And of course I realize that, to keep alive, one has to earn money. *You* should know that I realize that, Johnny. But I don't like the stuff. I *earn* money, but I don't *make* it. I don't even enjoy spending it, really. Spending makes me guilty. I've noticed there are two kinds of people—the ones who want to buy the cheapest and the ones who boast about buying the priciest. I fall into the first category, Johnny, just as you fall into the second."

"When I *had* any money, Delia—before the rand was devalued almost out of existence, and it was nearly all frozen in South Africa, anyway—I'm quite sure I never *boasted* about spending it."

"Oh, I don't know. Perhaps you still do. Look at those designers' initials you have on lots of your clothes. A customer paying to advertise a designer—it always seems a funny idea to me. Anyway, it's just a form of boasting about how much the clothes cost."

The muscle at the corner of Johnny's mouth became active: a tic. Bettina said, "I'm afraid *I* just buy the things I like."

GOING TOO FAR

Johnny's face calmed. He laughed. "Darling Bettina," he said, "I'm quite sure *that* invariably means the most expensive."

Delia said, "I've been holding forth." Humorously she turned down the corners of her mouth and cocked her head. In the silence, she laughed loudly. "I must go and piss," she said. "All that soda water!" Up she scrambled.

As she disappeared into the house, Johnny said, "I quite wish I was a very large dog. So that I could *savage* those rather thick ankles."

Bettina said, "I could never wish I were a dog."

"Oh, of course. You loathe them, don't you? I'd forgotten. Anyone would think you were a born Jew instead of a convert."

"A lapsed convert. Entirely lapsed since Max died. But do Jews dislike dogs particularly?"

"Oh, yes. I've often noticed. They think they're dirty."

"So do Muslims."

"Yes, of course. But one doesn't meet Muslims much, does one?"

"I certainly don't, with a name like Bernstein. Weren't you once great chums with some Persian millionaire, though?"

"Oh, Reza. Yes. That was in the good old days of the Shah. I haven't seen Reza for ages. He lost all his money after what Delia would probably call the glorious revolution."

"I'm quite sure she wouldn't. Delia detests militant Islam."

Johnny looked surprised. "But surely that's not the left-wing line? Zionist imperialism and so forth. . . ."

"Oh, she admits what a bad time the Palestinians have had. But she does it rather perfunctorily. It's not one of her

30

'things'. It can't be when she feels such a horror of Islam
—especially in connection with women, of course."

"You're tempting me irresistibly, Bettina. To announce
that I adore the ayatollahs. That I'm simply mad about
those mullahs. All for Allah, in fact."

"Fool!" Bettina laughed. Then she said, "But really,
Johnny, you mustn't bait her."

"Me? I'm behaving impeccably. When she burst onto
this terrace, the day before yesterday, wearing that red rag,
and said, 'I've had this swim-suit for fifteen years. Would
you believe it?' did I utter? Not a word!"

As Delia came out of the house, Johnny and Bettina
were both laughing. Delia's jaws were moving. Emerging
from under the vine she swallowed whatever was in her
mouth. "Tell me the joke," she said.

Bettina said, "We were talking about dogs."

"Dogs?"

"Yes. Johnny was wondering why I dislike them so
much."

Delia said, "Why do you?"

"It's not that I'm afraid of them." Between eyelids that
were almost closed, Bettina looked out to sea. "I don't
even feel they're especially dirty." After a glance at
Johnny, she looked back at the sea. "It's because of my
mother that I don't like them."

Johnny said, "Was she a dog? I never knew."

"Fool!" Bettina said again, with affection. Her tone
cooled: "Though one could certainly have described her as
a bitch."

Delia laughed, and said, "But how did she make you
dislike dogs?"

"Oh. Well, she adored them. She simply adored them."
Bettina paused. "She even called me after a dog."

Delia laughed again. "Shit! After a dog! I'm sure you've never told me that before."

"Woof, woof!" barked Johnny. "Bettina! Here, Bettina! Good doggie, then. Woof, woof, woof."

Bettina said, "After a dead dog." She spoke the words slowly, on a descending scale. There was silence: not even, on this still day, the sound of the sea.

"Bettina!" said Bettina. Her tone lightened: "My mother had a photograph of her by her bed, in a silver frame."

"Was it signed?" asked Johnny.

For a moment, Delia frowned, puzzled. Bettina laughed. "It's quite surprising, really, that it wasn't. My mother always talked about that dog as if it were human. More than human, perhaps. My mother preferred dogs to people."

"Was she one of those great tweedy ladies who slap their thighs and ride to hounds?" asked Johnny.

"Oh, not a bit like that. Very middle-class and urban. She wore little suits, the Chanel type—she couldn't afford the real thing. I've always loathed Chanel suits."

"Really?" Johnny sounded shocked.

"Mmm. The absolute perfection of mediocrity. So safe."

Delia said, "High fashion! Shit!"

Bettina said, "Bettina was a dachshund. Such an undignified breed for one's namesake—those sausage bodies and stumpy legs. My mother always had small dogs. She was a small woman. Apparently I took after my father. I don't remember him. He died when I was two. I've only seen a photograph. Though my mother didn't keep it by her bed, as she kept *Bettina's*." Bettina paused. Then, "My mother always said I'd grow too tall for ballet. She was right. Just as she was when I plucked my eyebrows. She said they'd never grow again, and they never did." Bettina hunched her shoulders. "Her cheeks were always mauve as if it were winter all year round."

Delia said, "It is, in England."

"She was a frozen woman. Like those rands of yours, Johnny. Dogs were the only thing that thawed her. *Bettina!* People used to say it was a funny name for an English girl. I suppose—though the alliteration's rather crude—that it goes better with Bernstein than it did with West-Walker."

"Yeah, West-Walker," said Delia. "You once told me that was your maiden name, and I always remembered it, because there was an arcade in Durban called West Walk."

"Really?" Johnny sounded weary.

"Yeah. Don't you remember?"

"No."

"West Walk. It was off West Street."

Johnny said, "That seems logical."

"It's probably still there. But you don't know?"

"No."

"Bettina!" said Bettina. "I've never told anyone about that before. I've always been ashamed of having been called after a dead dog. But it doesn't seem to matter any more, now."

Delia nodded, frowning. "You've worked through it, I suppose."

Johnny said, "Spare us the amateur psychology."

Delia said, "Psychology's more *your* line, I suppose, Johnny. Shit! Weren't you actually 'in analysis' at one time?"

"Only for a month. It was awfully boring."

"*In analysis*," Bettina repeated. "You make it sound as if he'd been in Scunthorpe, Dee-dee."

Johnny said, "Or one of those terrible towns in the Transvaal. Boksburg, Benoni, Brakpan—I wonder why they all begin with B."

"Though there are wonderful parts of the Transvaal," said Bettina. "I remember driving back to Natal from a farm in the highveld. It belonged to friends of Max's. Pine trees and waterfalls. Trout in the river. It was beautiful. But what I really liked was some country we drove through on the way back. Between Ermelo and Volksrust. Just flat pale land as far as one could see. Not a tree, not a building. There was just this flat pale land."

"Too austere for me," said Delia. "It's Natal I dream of. Oh, that green tropical tangle!"

"Ah," Johnny said, "those memories of tropical splendour. Rather vulgar, I always thought, even though we lived in Natal. But—"

"In the White Highlands," Delia broke in. "Nottingham Road and Mooi River. Frafly, frafly what-ho, doncher know. Retired English colonels slowly drinking themselves to death."

Johnny said, "Just like my dear departed father. Though he wasn't a colonel. But, *as I was going to say*, when you interrupted me, Delia, the Western Cape is the only part of South Africa that has ever really appealed to me. Those charming old Cape Dutch houses. The vineyards. Those enormous oak trees. The hundreds of wild flowers. So awfully civilized."

"Insipid," said Delia. "Too much like Europe."

"That's just what I said. It's civilized."

34

Delia said, "Shit! I suppose you'll start talking about 'white civilization' any minute now."

"I wouldn't dream of using such an expression. It's a positive trademark of the barbarous Boers."

Delia said, "My mother was half Afrikaans. But that's not what bothers me when you talk like that. It's that being anti-Afrikaans is so crass. Quite different from being anti-apartheid. Afrikaners are more deeply rooted in the country than English-speaking people are."

Johnny said, "I'll have you know that my great-grandfather arrived in Durban before there was even a proper port. He had to be carried ashore on the back of a Zulu."

"And the family has been sitting on the Zulus' backs ever since, hey? Anyway, the Afrikaners' roots go back further. They're deeper than that. The Afrikaners belong to Africa."

"Perhaps that's what I find so awful about them. And don't start calling me *racist*, Delia. You *can't*, in the circumstances. Since the Boers are white, not black."

"I can certainly call you a chauvinist."

"You don't understand. It's the whole bloody continent I can't bear." He leant forward, staring out towards the three rocks. His Adam's apple jerked as he swallowed. The muscle at the corner of his mouth twitched. "*Bloody* continent. That's what I said, and I meant it literally. I was thinking. While I was swimming. About what you said, Bettina. About the blood. About the drops of blood— from Medusa's head, weren't they, her severed head? —falling on Africa and turning into snakes. Blood falling instead of rain, till the dry earth's soaked with it. The ground becomes fertile, but it grows snakes instead of crops. The first you see of them is their tongues, like little forked seedlings. But then the blunt heads follow, weaving in the air, and the bodies writhe up after them. The snakes slither along the ground. Some slide up the trunks of trees. Then they lie along the branches or hang limply over them. And sometimes they drop down. Oh, what a horror!"

One of his hands was trembling. He gripped the side of the stretcher. "And have you seen those dreadful carvings in black wood? People and things—heaven knows what long-faced things—entwined like snakes. Limbs merging with each other, making more snakes. Did you know that a snake *slimes* its prey? It covers it with slime to make it ready for gorging." Johnny bowed his head, and pressed his palms against his cheekbones. His fingers were clasped round his skull.

Delia's mouth had opened, and Bettina gave her a quelling glance. But Delia did not look righteous; she looked astonished.

"Oh, Johnny, man, how weird," she said. "What weird ideas you have. All that blood, and all those snakes and stuff. Don't you remember the Valley of a Thousand Hills? The little round hills like plum-puddings, and the little round thatched huts. In the evening there's woodsmoke, and dogs are barking, and people call to each other from far away. The voices rise from the huts, and sometimes there's singing. Sad, but so strong and rich and generous. African singing! Oh, Johnny, Africa has so much to tell us. Through music, through song, through poetry.

"*There are those who are born of the sun*
Who, by their lips give life to the withered leaf.

> *But others are the spirit of the forest,*
> *They penetrate the root of the ancient tree."*

While Delia talked and recited, Johnny had calmed down. Now he was lying back again, his arms folded over his chest. "I presume you're quoting from some *poem*," he said, "even though it doesn't rhyme."

"Yeah. It's an African poem. It's called, 'Return of the Golden Age'."

Johnny said, "Golden Age, indeed! An *African* poem! Books by blacks. Books about blacks. What's the point? *They* don't read, and whites aren't interested. I'm not, anyway. When I read, I want to be entertained, and, to me, black's not beautiful: it's *boring*. Really, Delia, it's sad, isn't it, *you* thinking the country so wonderful, and not being allowed in? While *I* positively drag myself there, at Christmas, to see my dear mama—and to spend a little of my depleted money. And Bettina never goes back and doesn't want to. Lucky Bettina! *She* got her money out in time."

"Max did," said Bettina. "He always knew how things were going to develop. For years and years he'd been moving his money out."

"African money," Delia murmured.

Johnny said, "For heaven's sake, let's stop talking about Africa." He paused, then, looking out to sea, "Though I did rather like Marrakesh when I went there. But of course that's Arab, not African. Islamic. So much, much more glamorous."

Delia let out a blast of breath. "Shit! Trust you, Johnny! Trust you to fall for Islam! The only system in the world that's as bad as apartheid. Well, it *is* apartheid. Women

37

totally shut away—even Verwoerd never dreamed of segregation on *that* scale. And at least blacks in South Africa can *wear* what they want. They aren't muzzled and covered in *shrouds*. And they can drive cars. Women can't in Saudi Arabia. I'd rather die than visit an Islamic country. I think they should all be boycotted."

Johnny said, "Oh God, there she goes again. *Another* boycott!"

Bettina said, "Be realistic, Dee-dee, darling. Think of all that oil. A boycott doesn't stand a chance. Stick to South Africa. Though I feel uranium may elude you."

Mouth open, Delia leant forward. But Bettina, spreading the fingers of both hands in the air, to deter her, turned to Johnny: "Pour me another drink, please, darling. I haven't finished this one, but the sparkle's gone, and it's tepid, too."

"Of course!" Up he bounded. "Same again?"

"No. No, I don't think so. What *do* I feel like?" Brooding, she rested her right elbow on her crossed right knee; her chin was cupped in her hand. She drooped. The sleeve of her kaftan, falling back, was a calyx: from it emerged her pale attenuate arm.

Now both Delia—plans for speech manifestly abandoned—and Johnny—looking down at Bettina's dark-brown hair and her dead-white, dead-straight centre parting—seemed suspended. Then Johnny said, "That divine scent of yours, Bettina. *Bain de Champagne*. It's flowery, yet it's not a bit sickly. Do you know, I was in some theatre in London, and I smelt it, and I swung round, thinking, 'Here's darling Bettina!' But it was just some dreary hag. A fake, an impostor! I felt she should be prosecuted."

Bettina straightened. She smiled. She snapped her

fingers. "Champagne!" she said. "*That*'s what I feel like. A glass of champagne."

Delia's eyes opened wide. "Champagne!" she exclaimed in a breathy whisper.

"Just the thing!" said Johnny. "It almost always is." He picked up Bettina's glass, still a third full, and moved briskly under the vine and into the house.

Bettina said, "The way you said 'Champagne!', Deedee! You sounded like an old-fashioned child saying, 'Father Christmas!'"

"I love champagne."

Bettina smiled. "I would have thought you'd disapprove of it."

"Well, of course it is a bit extravagant of you, always drinking French wine."

Bettina said, "I've never acquired the taste for retsina."

"Anyway, to hell with it. Kill-joy, wet blanket, spoilsport! I'm sure Johnny thinks of me like that, but—shit! —I don't expect it from you. Marxists aren't necessarily puritans, you know. A lot of us enjoy having a good time. Champagne's so festive, and I've always loved a party. Dancing, in the old days, as well as drinking."

"Yes, I remember how we used to put on 'The Little Shoemaker', towards the end of an evening, and you'd whirl, whirl, faster and faster, all by yourself."

"Yeah! Shit! 'The Little Shoemaker'! It was one of my 'things', dancing to that record. There was a summer night at an old house at Kloof. A wooden veranda, with a light-bulb hanging on a brown flex. The flying ants threw themselves against the light and burnt their wings. I remember their bodies crunching under my feet as I danced to 'The Little Shoemaker'."

"You danced rather well."

"Mmm. When I'd had enough to drink. Enough to have stopped feeling shy and self-conscious. And I always liked dancing alone. Thank goodness those awful ballroom dances—the waltz and foxtrot, and so on—were over before our time!"

"Almost over. Max and his friends still did those dances. I quite enjoyed them."

"Well, of course, you'd trained as a dancer."

"Ballroom dancing is quite different from ballet."

"It's a shame you got too tall."

"Yes . . . in a way. But, in any case, I don't think I would have been good enough."

"To be a prima ballerina, you mean?"

"What else?"

Johnny came out of the house, carrying a tray which he put down on the round pine table.

Delia said, "The perfect butler—our Johnny!"

"Ganymede, the cup-bearer," Bettina murmured.

On the tray a bottle of champagne lolled among ice in a silver bucket. Beside it were three champagne flutes. Seeing them, Delia called out loudly, "None for me, remember!"

"OK, OK," said Johnny. "I brought the extra glass just in case champagne was an exception to your rule. To save myself another journey."

After a moment, Delia said, "Champagne glasses used to be round and shallow, didn't they?"

Johnny said, "They haven't been like that for years."

"Shows how seldom I've drunk champagne. Why did they change them?"

Johnny said, "In shallow glasses, the effervescence dies down more quickly."

"Sounds silly to me. Probably just a way of making

people buy new glasses. Consumerism! Shit! I don't feel things like that should be changed. Things like champagne glasses. They have special associations."

"The voice of the revolution speaks," said Johnny, but Delia made no response. With close attention she was watching him open the bottle.

Pop went the cork. Without spilling a drop, Johnny poured foam into one of the glasses. "The perfect butler," Delia said again. "Jeeves in person!"

Johnny said, "Jeeves wasn't a butler. He was a valet."

He carried the two filled glasses over to Bettina. Handing her one, he said, "Amazingly good health!"

"Mmm." She closed her eyes, opened them again. "Health, Johnny." They both drank.

Bettina said, "And what about you, Dee-dee? Isn't there anything you'd like?"

"No, I don't think. . . ." But then she glanced at Johnny, resettling on his stretcher, glass in hand. She said, "Well, perhaps I'll have some of that Perrier of yours, after all. More partyish. More in the champagne mood."

She didn't move, nor did Johnny. After a moment, Bettina said, "Johnny, would you be very sweet, and fetch Delia some Perrier?"

He said, "Of course, darling. Anything for you." His face flickered as he stood up. He crossed the terrace, his shoulders tense. He put down his champagne glass on the table in the shade, and went indoors.

A pause. Then Delia said, "Funny he should hate snakes when he's so like one. Dry and slithery." She rummaged in her basket, and found another roll of peppermints. Unwrapping it, she said, "How I *wish*. . . ." Instead of finishing the sentence, she put two more peppermints in her mouth. Then she announced, "Nearly six months, now!"

Bettina had slumped a little in her chair. She was looking down at the glass in her hand; it rested on the full curve of her stomach. Sounding pre-occupied, she said, "Six months?"

"Since I gave up." Delia laughed her loud laugh. "The drink, you know."

Bettina said, "Oh, yes. Amazing. Six months. A long time." She paused. "Or it can seem a very short time."

"Well, it certainly hasn't seemed short to me. It seems to have gone on for ever. Shit!" She gave a big sigh. "How I miss it! When you drink, there's always something to look forward to."

Bettina looked up. She said, "No, seriously, Dee-dee, I think it's marvellous. Most impressive."

Johnny came out of the house, twisting off the cap of a Perrier bottle. He said, "Do you want ice, Delia? It's straight from the fridge."

"Yeah," said Delia. Then, "Please. *And* a slice of lemon. If it's not too much trouble." To Bettina she said, "I miss it every single day."

"Miss what?" asked Johnny, sawing off a slice of lemon. He put it in one of the squat tumblers, poured Perrier, dropped in a single cube of ice: plop. "Our beloved homeland, perchance?"

Delia hesitated. Then she said, "No I was talking about drink, Johnny. About the booze, the grog, the tipple."

Bettina said, "Euripides called it 'our only cure for the weariness of life'. It's the gift of Dionysus. Dionysus the benevolent, Dionysus the ruthless."

"Can one be both?" asked Johnny, stooping to put Delia's drink down beside her. Back at the stretcher, he sank onto it with a deep dramatic sigh.

Bettina said, "But of course one can. I'd say that benevolence and ruthlessness are almost inseparable. Certainly they were in Dionysus. He taught people how to grow crops and get honey as well as how to make wine. But at the same time he punished people implacably if they didn't respect his divinity. Look what happened to Pentheus."

"Pentheus?" said Delia. "I don't know about him."

"He was a king of Thebes. He detested the god Dionysus and his rites. He denied his divinity, and forbade the Thebans to worship him. When Dionysus came to Thebes on a visit, Pentheus put him in jail. And even when the prison doors opened of their own accord to let him out, Pentheus wasn't convinced or converted. In fact, it just made him angrier. He told his soldiers to go out into the countryside and destroy the god's worshippers: the Bacchae, the maenads or possessed ones. And they—the maenads—included Pentheus's own mother and aunts.

"At that point Dionysus intervened. He used his divine power to fill Pentheus with an obsessive longing to watch the maenads' rites—their evil rites, as Pentheus thought them. He persuaded Pentheus to disguise himself as a woman."

"A king in drag!" said Johnny. "The perfect drag queen!"

"Pentheus dressed up in a long robe and a headband. He wrapped himself in a dappled fawnskin. Guided by Dionysus, he went into the country and hid in a pine tree.

"The women, the maenads, had been rejoicing quite

43

innocently until then, dancing, wreathing their heads with garlands, feeding young animals on their own breast-milk."

"Ugh!" said Johnny.

"And they had only to strike or touch the earth, and out flowed water or wine or milk or honey. But then Dionysus maddened them. He guided them to Pentheus.

"Imagine those women, those maenads running over the country with their wild hair and their wild dazed eyes. They carried big branches and bowls of wine. They moved faster than wild animals—they picked up deer and wildcats and whirled them in the air. They didn't feel the rough ground beneath their feet, for their feet hardly seemed to touch it as they ran. Their pleated tunics moved to the rhythm of their bodies. When they reached the great tree where Pentheus was hiding they tore it up by its roots. Then, led by the mother of Pentheus—she was so possessed that she didn't recognize her own son—they tore him to pieces. His bones were stripped bare. The women's hands were drenched in blood. Pentheus shrieked until the moment of death, and all the time the women howled with joy. They were playing ball with lumps of his flesh. Pieces of him were scattered among the rocks and in the woods. But his head was carried back to Thebes in triumph by his mother. She thought it was a lion's head. Until she was dispossessed. The god deserted her, and then at last she realized what she'd done."

There was a silence. "So what happened then?" said Delia.

"Everyone was wretched and accursed. The god departed, dooming the city and its inhabitants. The mother of Pentheus went into miserable exile."

Delia exclaimed, "But that's not fair! The god had made

44

her do it. Shit, when she killed her son she was doing what the god wanted.''

Bettina said, ''Things aren't 'fair', Delia.''

There was another silence. Then Delia said. ''The women. The maenads. Were they drunk or mad?''

Bettina said, ''They were possessed.''

''You aren't answering my question.''

Bettina said, ''How can I?'' Then, ''There are marvellous paintings of maenads on Greek vases. As a matter of fact I've got a maenad cup myself. My most precious possession. I'm not all that keen on possessions nowadays, but I really love that cup.''

Johnny, lying back on the stretcher, took a sip of champagne. He smiled. ''What did he look like—Dionysus?''

''Oh, sometimes he was a beautiful youth with flowing curls and a white skin. And sometimes he was a decrepit old man—to show that too much wine makes people prematurely old. It destroys them.''

Delia said, ''It's true what you've been saying. It's all true. Drink cures the weariness of life—and yet it also leads to misery and madness and destruction.''

''In excess,'' said Bettina.

Johnny sighed. ''All this sounds terribly *heavy*, to me. I mean I like the booze, but I can't see that it's so ecstatic. Or so tragic, either.'' He drank the last drops in his glass. ''More champagne, Bettina?''

''Yes, please.''

He took his glass and Bettina's over to the tray. Delia said, ''And yet you just admitted that your father *died* of drink, Johnny.''

Holding the bottle, he looked up. Then he started to pour the wine. ''Oh, well,'' he said, ''there was nothing tragic about that. It was just dull. Like a leaking tap goes drip, drip, drip, my dear departed daddy went sip, sip, sip." He gave Bettina her glass, and went back to the stretcher. "Anyway," he said, "I can take the stuff or leave it."

Delia said, "Well, aren't you lucky, Johnny! That's just what I can't do. In the sense you mean. Though, in another sense, it's all I can do. Take it or leave it. One or the other. I have to choose."

Johnny said, "That sounds awfully *extreme*, to me."

Bettina said, "Delia *is* extreme."

Delia laughed. "Shit—too true!"

"But I mean, Delia," Johnny persisted, "you've always drunk a lot. It was one of your 'things', as you'd put it. I always thought you were having a good time."

"Oh, I was." She nodded with vigour. "I often was."

"Then why stop? You know, I think you used to be *jollier*. When you drank a bit."

Delia laughed very loudly. "Jollier! Shit—less boring, you mean!" She took two more peppermints from the roll. She said, "Well, at least, drink is better than drugs."

Johnny shrugged. "You think so? Doing drugs can be quite fun. Nice little ups and downs, and no hangovers."

"*Doing* them, indeed! Shit—they're *addictive*."

"Not all of them—and no more than drink, as you describe it."

Delia shrugged. She fumbled in her basket, pulled out a crumpled handkerchief, mopped her forehead. "It's certainly hot," she said to Bettina.

Bettina said, "I don't know how you two can bear it. Lying in the sun, hour after hour." She glanced upwards, then looked out to sea. She said, "Imagine Icarus falling from the sky. His father, Daedalus made wings for them

46

both. He cemented the wings with wax. Icarus flew too close to the sun, and the wax melted. He fell into the sea and drowned."

"Splash! Kerplonk!" exclaimed Johnny. Then, "Glup, glup, glup." He imitated a drowning person swallowing water.

"Daedalus was wise," said Bettina. "He kept his distance, and survived." She added, "He was an artist."

"I shall survive, too," said Johnny. "I find the sun relaxing. But of course I always wear my dark glasses."

"I hate dark glasses." Delia squinted up at the sky. "They drain the life out of the way things look. They remind me of horrible Latin-American dictators. And people use them as a disguise. To hide their real feelings."

"Of course now they're saying the sun can give one cancer." Johnny's tone was fretful. "And we always used to think it was so healthy."

Delia said, "Shit! Everything's supposed to give one cancer now."

"Not drink," said Johnny.

"Oh, they'll get around to that. Then I'll *have to* take it up again. Just to show them."

"Delia you're so childish." Bettina's tone was cool. "Show them what?"

"That I don't care."

Bettina said, "Don't care was made to care."

Johnny said, "I must say it sounds awfully strange to me. Taking up drink to cock a snook at the doctors, but not so as to have fun."

"Fun!" said Delia. "But it stopped being fun. It became something different. I couldn't justify it in the way I'd always been able to. Because—at one time—it really was a good thing. It freed me. As being overweight did. It stopped me getting involved with the wrong kind of man."

Johnny laughed. "What kind's *that*?"

"The kind that wants a woman to be a credit to him."

Now Bettina laughed. "Don't they all?"

"Perhaps they do. One always hopes for someone who's not concerned with the surface. Someone who's looking for something deeper."

Johnny said, "Someone who'll love you for your beautiful soul?"

Delia said, "Oh, ha ha. But, yeah, that sort of thing. Though of course I don't believe in the soul. But probably all men just want trophies. Proofs of success, like silver cups for sport. A woman who drinks a lot can't be that. Ellis used to hate it when I got drunk."

Bettina said, "You're the only woman I know who refers to her ex-husband by his surname."

"Like a peer's signature," said Johnny. "I'd love to sign things simply 'Fairfield'."

Delia said to Bettina, "Shit! What do you expect me to call him— *Trev*?"

"No," said Bettina. "But you could say Trevor."

"Trevor's a pretty ghastly name," said Johnny. "Almost as bad as Darren."

Delia said to Bettina, "I think it's very civilized of me to call him Ellis." Her voice rose. "Instead of calling him that filthy swine. I can't *bear* him. Foul, filthy, fucking swine!" Grabbing her handkerchief, she stumbled up, and ran —her bare feet thudding on the tiles—into the house.

"Drama!" said Johnny. "And how red her face went. Almost purple."

"It's all my fault," Bettina said. "I wasn't thinking."

Johnny said, "*She* raised the subject. Of *Ellis*. It was perfectly reasonable of you to point out that it's ridiculous for her to call him that."

"I shouldn't have. I should have distracted her. You can't blame her for feeling strongly about him. After all, he stole her child."

"Surely that's an exaggeration. If she hadn't got mixed up with those saboteurs, and had to flee the country, it would never have happened."

"It isn't even as if he really loves the child. He's married again, and the new wife doesn't want her. I don't think he does either. Anyway, he's dumped her with Delia's dreadful parents."

"Are they really so dreadful?"

"Terribly respectable and conventional. And extraordinarily religious. They write to Delia once a year, at Christmas, telling her to come to Jesus."

Johnny laughed. "What a hope!"

"They won't let her communicate with her daughter at all. I've been wishing lately that I could have that child kidnapped."

"*Kidnapped*, Bettina?"

"Mmm. There's never been any legal possibility of getting her out. The South African courts would support Trevor all the way. But if the child were kidnapped and brought to England, Trevor wouldn't stand a chance of getting her back. Oh, I don't know. Perhaps I should just give Delia a lot of money"—she glanced sideways at Johnny—"and let her decide."

"Give Delia a lot of money?" Johnny sounded astonished and affronted. After a moment, he said, "But wouldn't she just hand it over to *the cause*. Surely, it's quite against those principles of hers to spend it on her own concerns. *African* money—didn't you hear her call your money that?"

"Yes. In a way, of course, it's true."

"Oh, *Bettina*! How can you say so, darling? Max worked hard for that money."

"Mmm. Yes, Max worked hard." There was a pause. Bettina said, "Of course that child isn't a child any more. She must be nearly thirteen."

"My God! A terrible teenager! If you ask me, Delia's well out of it. Can you picture her with a teenage daughter? I can just hear them yelling at each other. 'Mother, come to Jesus.' 'Daughter, come to Marx.'"

"You're callous, Johnny." But Bettina smiled.

"What's the daughter called?"

"Eleanor. After Marx's daughter. But I don't think Delia told Trevor that."

"Eleanor Ellis!"

"Almost as schmaltzy as Bettina Bernstein."

Johnny laughed. "I wonder what she looks like—that Eleanor Ellis. I seem to remember that Trevor was rather good-looking. Let's hope she takes after *him*."

"Oh, really, Johnny. Delia's very handsome."

"That limp, snaky hair. . . ."

"Lovely and straight!" Bettina sounded wistful.

"You've got a fetish about that, darling. Always having yours straightened, just like the blacks. Can't think why you bother."

"I like to look *soignée*."

"And you *do*. As you well know. Anyway, apart from the hair, and that more than ample figure, I think she's got a face like a plate. A big round pottery plate. Rather coarse pottery, too. With food on it, for the features. Those doggy eyes: two soggy prunes. Mouth: an overripe tomato, *oozing*—her lipstick's always smudged. Nose: a potato, with two holes gouged in it for those rocking-horse nostrils."

"You're so bitchy, Johnny. Anyway, *I* admire her. Quite apart from her appearance, she's got such character, such stamina. You know, this giving up drink is a major achievement."

"A major bore. Major Delia. Perhaps she should join the Salvation Army."

Bettina said, "Delia is the best of us."

"Oh, *Bettina*!"

"I must go and see how she is." But as Bettina straightened, to stand, and Johnny sat upright—with open mouth, as if about to speak—Delia came out of the house. The skin round her eyes was blotched; her handkerchief was balled in her hand. Again, her jaws were moving. She swallowed.

"Don't know what came over me, as they say!" A very loud, abrupt laugh. "What were we talking about before Ellis upset my apple-cart?"

Johnny lay back again on the stretcher. "Your drink problem," he said.

Bettina frowned. Delia, however, seemed unperturbed. "Yeah, that's right," she said. "How drink stopped being fun when it started to take over."

Johnny said "That sounds just like love."

"More like lust. Shit! A kidnapper carrying me off to a brothel I might never be able to escape from."

Johnny said, "The white slave-traffic. . . ."

"I found I was spending five days at a time drinking when it got hold of me. Down, down, down."

Johnny said, "You talk as if it were alive."

"I feel it is. Like that kidnapper. Or a vampire—shit! *Thirsting* for me. Wanting to drink my blood."

"Awfully romantic. Like something out of Edgar Allan Poe."

Delia said, "He was an alcoholic, of course." She laughed. "Like so many of the best people."

"Scott Fitzgerald," murmured Bettina.

"Dylan Thomas," said Delia. "Jack London."

"Jean Rhys," said Bettina. "Modigliani."

"How you reel them off—those big names," said Johnny. "Do you remember that wonderful old movie, *A Star is Born*? The Judy Garland version. James Mason played the drunk. He committed suicide by swimming out to sea. Awfully noble. Terribly camp."

"Fearfully difficult," said Delia. "Almost impossible. Shit! I can't imagine letting myself drown. My will to live would blaze up at the last minute, and I'd turn round and struggle back to shore."

"But one couldn't if one were really exhausted," said Bettina. "That would be the way to make sure. Just swim on and on, until one had gone too far. Until one was too tired to get back, even if one wanted to."

"Glup, glup, glup." Again Johnny did his imitation of someone drowning.

Delia said, "I suppose your father killed himself more gradually than that."

"How melodramatic, Delia—"

She interrupted: "It was you who said he drank himself to death."

"Yes, well—but I'm sure *he* didn't think of it like that. Of course the doctor told him he must cut down, but my father said he was just an old fuss-pot—rather your attitude to the medical profession, Delia. Anyway, the whole scene was tremendously tedious. As I said before, he just sat there, sipping. Those long, lethal colonial whisky-and-sodas. Sometimes he muttered to himself. He had this old tag he'd repeat, over and over, as the evening wore on. 'Love and affection. Love and affection.' *Ugh*—so maudlin! And so frightfully boring for my poor mama and me."

"Oh, too frafly, frafly, I'm sure!" said Delia. "What about your elder sister?"

"My dull elder sister wasn't there. She was married to her even duller husband. Living in deadly Port Elizabeth."

Delia said, "Didn't your mother try to do anything about your father's drinking?"

"What do you suggest she could have done?" The pitch of Johnny's voice rose as he said this.

"Johnny, a drop more champagne, please," said Bettina."

"Awfully good idea!" He leapt up.

Bettina said, "The worst drunk I ever knew was Micky van Rooyen."

"Short back and sides, leather jacket, walked like a sailor. Heave ho, my hearties!" Johnny, taking Bettina's glass, laughed. "Amazingly butch!"

"An artist, wasn't she?" said Delia.

Bettina said, "Yes, I took painting-lessons from her. And she used to give me rides on the back of her motor-bike at night. Bouncing over the Berea, while, down below, the lights of Durban were blinking madly!"

"Zoom, zoom," said Johnny, pouring wine.

"Max was furious when he found out. He said I might have been killed."

"Or worse, darling." Johnny smiled as he handed Bettina her glass.

She took a sip. "Micky could have been a splendid painter. But drink was her undoing. She couldn't give it up . . . she wouldn't seriously try. Apart from her addiction to it, it was so tied up with her life-style. That dreary *vie de bohème*. Even today a few old painters and poets believe in that quaint dream. They see it as part of the mystique of art. Living in squalor. Not paying the rent—even if one has the money—because it's *bourgeois*. And, of course, getting drunk all the time."

"Awfully tatty." Johnny rearranged himself on the stretcher.

"Rejecting a sick society's values?" Delia's tone was uncertain. "A degree of integrity? A refusal to compromise?"

"*No*," said Bettina. "Squalor produces torpor and despair. If you don't pay the rent, the landlord turns you out. If you're drunk you can't work—and you scarcely can with a hangover. All such a waste of time. Artists shouldn't waste their time. Oh, what a lot of time Micky wasted. '*God verdom*, I was pissed as a fiddler's bitch last night.' She'd say it with such pride, seeing the same vision of herself as she saw when she rode that motor-bike. Daredevil Mick! And her hand would shake so much that she couldn't hold a paintbrush. She'd have to take a swig of brandy to steady it. Naturally she couldn't produce serious work. To keep alive—and buy brandy—she had to do things that betrayed her integrity more than being *bourgeois* ever could have done. She used to paint hack watercolours of rickshaws and Zulu kraals for tourists. 'Fuckin' rickshaws and *rondavels* for the *rooineks*,' she'd say. And she'd always add, 'Of course I don't *sign* them.' But it was just as much a waste of time as if she had. And a waste of *her*. Cheapening. Debasing. In the end, her liver gave up the struggle. *She* didn't. What a battle! I was ignorant in those days. And stupid. I imagined that dying was something peaceful. I thought one would feel *sleepy*. How shocked I was by Micky's raging deathbed."

"You were there?" Johnny tilted up his chin.

"She asked for me." Bettina looked out to sea.

Delia was pulling at her crumpled handkerchief, straightening it. "Shit—she sounds fine in a way. Brave."

Bettina said, "Not brave enough to sacrifice her self-image to her art. *Not brave enough.*"

"How ruthless you sound, darling." Johnny spoke with relish.

Delia looped one corner of her handkerchief into a knot, and pulled it tight. Studying it, she said, "The finest person I ever knew was a drunk. He changed my life."

"Goodness! Tell us more," said Johnny.

"He was an assistant lecturer at varsity—until they fired him. Politics was his subject, but sometimes he helped out with Economics, too—if someone was ill or had to go away. He was in his fifties—old, I thought then. And of course he *was* old, to be only an assistant lecturer. But he was unreliable. Because of the drinking. All the same, he was brilliant, and they made use of him as long as they could."

"Edward Bone," said Johnny. "Tall. Heavy eyebrows. Dark-red face. I used to see him shambling round the campus."

"Yeah. That was him. That was him. Shit!—I often think he was the first person I ever really talked to. He was certainly the first person I ever really drank with."

"Ah," said Johnny.

"He was a Marxist."

The sound Johnny made was just too low to be a groan.

"He'd become one in the 1930s at Cambridge. He never changed. He had a splendid scorn of capitalism."

"I'm surprised he didn't join the Foreign Office and become a Russian spy," said Johnny. "Like all the others did."

"Shit! Edward was far too indiscreet and impulsive to have been a spy. Any more than he could have been a diplomat. Though he was in the Colonial Service for a bit, just after the war."

Johnny said, "I suppose he'd been a pacifist."

"You've got your political lines crossed. Absolutely not! He won all sorts of medals and became a colonel. Anyway, when he joined the Colonial Service he was sent to the West Indies. He got drunk at a banquet, and made a rude speech about colour prejudice in the British Empire. Of course, they got rid of him. Then his wife left him. After that . . . he drifted."

"To South Africa?" said Johnny. "Most unsuitable, I'd have thought."

"He thought so, too. But he'd nearly touched bottom when he met the owner of some South African paper company who was on a visit to London. A great snob—he was impressed by Edward's manner, which was sometimes rather grand, and his background. A first at Cambridge and all that, doncher know! And Edward could be very charming. Anyway, this man persuaded him to come out and take a job. 'Product Manager,' I think he was called. 'Four different-coloured toilet papers—a perfect example of the sheer idiocy of capitalism!' Edward said that, drunk, in a speech at his first sales conference."

Johnny said, "Surely he didn't call it *toilet* paper?"

"Probably he didn't, Johnny. He probably said whatever *you* say. Is the posh term 'bog' paper or 'loo' paper?

But I'm helluva sure he didn't say it for the reasons you do. It would have been just out of habit. In any case, I don't remember. Because it isn't important to me. Any more than it would have been to him." Delia tugged another knot tight in her handkerchief. She said, "The point is that he lost his job."

"And got washed up at 'varsity', as you call it. On a tide of booze."

Delia said, "I admired him so much. I still do. He was scathing about capitalism, and about anything pretentious, but he could be very kind. He was kind to me."

"Aha!"

"Oh shit, Johnny. Trust you! It wasn't anything like that. It was *pure*, what there was between us."

"Goodness!"

"Pure—and very important. He made me understand the message of history."

"Goodness!"

"He used to come and see me sometimes, after I was married. We'd talk and talk."

"And drink and drink?"

"Yeah, that's right. He'd been fired from varsity by then. He took a job as commissionaire at the big cinema opposite the library—that Tudor-style cinema where the ceiling was a fake sky, with stars that twinkled. He wore a braided uniform with a peaked hat, and when any of the profs from varsity went there, he used to bow and sweep off the hat." Delia laughed. "It embarrassed the hell out of them. He'd still got that job when I had to leave the country."

Johnny said, "I'm sure he applauded your subversive activities!"

"Oh, I didn't talk to him about my political work." Delia sounded shocked. "All the same, he knew that he'd influenced my ideas. 'You taught me to think,' I told him. That was one of the last times we met, and I'm so glad I said it. I wanted to write to him after I reached England, but I thought that hearing from me might put him in danger. They could have been opening his mail, you know. Then I learnt that he'd died. Shit!"

Johnny said, "Another martyr to cirrhosis."

"Waste!" Bettina sounded fierce. She was sitting low in her chair. "Waste!"

"Yeah," said Delia. "Yeah, I know. And I have to agree, of course. But I feel Edward was brave, just as I feel that your friend Micky was."

"Waste. Nothing but waste," said Bettina.

Now, in a silence, Delia, who had tied four knots in her handkerchief, started to untie them. She said, "Piss artists."

Johnny laughed.

Delia said, "Yeah, I know that sounds funny. But I've always thought it was one of those phrases with a deeper meaning. Shit—when some people devote themselves to drink, it's a kind of life's work. Exhausting work. Work that burns them out. Moments of, well, ecstasy, paid for with hours of agony. Piss artists suffer—you can see that from the way it marks their faces. Piss artists are serious, just as real artists are. Other people can go on drinking and drinking for years. They float on the surface and they never sink. Even though drinking's their main occupation, they don't drown. The piss artists are different. Usually they're people who have wanted to do something else, something important. But either they've lacked the stamina, or they've lacked the gift itself."

Johnny said, "So they spend their time getting plastered?"

"Yeah."

"Nonsense," said Bettina. "At first, drink's an excuse for failure, and then failure's an excuse for drink. Soon —anything becomes an excuse for drinking." Now Bettina—blue-white—sat up straight. "I feel a bit tired," she said. "I think I'll have a little rest." She looked at her watch. "Half-past twelve. We don't need to eat before half-past two, do we?"

Johnny said, "Darling, of course not." Simultaneously, Delia's face showed disappointment. But, at once, she adjusted her expression to a grin. "Of course not," she echoed.

Bettina rested her hands—the silvered nails glinted—on the arms of her chair. Then, standing, she said, "Everything's ready for lunch."

"Oh, I *saw*," said Delia. "In the fridge. Such lovely things. The most beautiful potato salad. . . ."

Johnny said, "Delia, have you, by any chance, been *picking*?"

A flush rose from Delia's neck to her forehead. "I don't know what you mean," she said. Then, "Really, Bettina, I can't think how you do it. Delicious meals always ready. Everything so perfectly clean and tidy."

Bettina, under the vine now, turned her head. "Oh, it's quite simple. I'm an early riser. And this house is easy to look after."

"All those *gadgets*—shit!" Delia sounded impressed, if perhaps not approving.

"It was terribly expensive, bringing electricity here, from the town," said Bettina. "I might as well make use of it. Though it's always fusing. I'm getting quite good at dealing with fuses, but I have to get an electrician out here at least once a month."

"No blacks around," said Johnny. "Gadgets are a good idea. Anyway, they're more efficient. Cheaper to run, too. The initial investment pays off awfully quickly."

Going into the house, Bettina, without turning, said, "Oh, you two!" She sounded weary.

But Delia laughed. "Shit, Johnny, man," she said, her tone good-natured. "Always trying to get a rise out of me, hey?"

Johnny did not look pleased by this response. He lit a cigarette. Then, after a moment, he said, "Bettina gets tired so easily now. In times past she never flagged. 'A little rest'!—she would have had a fit if anyone had suggested such a thing."

Delia said, "That's right. She never used to flag in the old days, and she never expected anyone else to. She was quite a puritan about it. She made you feel guilty whenever you were doing nothing. I remember how she used to disapprove of sunbathing. It wasn't because of the fact that she didn't enjoy it herself. It was because it was so 'mindless'—that's what she used to say. And when she took me to France that time, we never stopped sightseeing. She couldn't bear just sitting around in cafés." Delia sighed. Then, "She was talking this morning about all those courses she took at varsity. Shit! And of course there was the ballet, before we knew her. And then all those years when she studied painting. You know, I thought she really wanted to be a painter, and I thought she was really talented. But she seems to have given that up."

Johnny said, "She certainly hasn't done any painting since I've been here."

Delia said, "And there don't seem to be any of her

pictures around—except one lovely little watercolour in my bathroom, of all places."

"Yes," Johnny said, "I noticed that one. I had the room you're in"—he gestured towards the window with the blue awning—"before you came."

"Sorry about that, Johnny. I didn't know you'd had to clear out."

"Oh, the room I'm in now is really just as nice. Bettina simply felt you ought to have the best *view* as you're here for such a short time." He smiled. "I'll move back when you've gone. But anyway, apart from that watercolour, there isn't a single picture anywhere. By anyone at all—let alone by her." He paused. "It's awfully odd to see all these naked walls in a house of Bettina's. She's always had masses of pictures everywhere."

"Yeah." Delia unwrapped two peppermints and put them in her mouth. She said, "I'm not surprised she gets tired during the day. She talks about early rising, but as far as I can make out, she hardly sleeps at night. If ever I wake up, the light's on out here, or I hear her wandering about the house. Like a ghost. She's so pale. She's always been pale, but never so pale as this."

Johnny said, "Never so thin, either."

"Except around the middle. Her stomach, you know."

"I haven't noticed," Johnny said coldly.

"It almost looks as if she was a few months pregnant."

Johnny gagged. His hand jerked up to the base of his throat. He said, "Oh, really, Delia, you're quite disgusting."

Delia looked indignant. "Shit! I didn't mean to be. Shit! I don't know what's disgusting about being pregnant. Anyway—shit!—I never meant to imply that Bettina is. I just said her stomach looks that way."

"I haven't noticed," Johnny repeated, louder.

Delia shrugged. "It's just middle-aged spread, I suppose."

"Middle-aged, indeed!" His tone was petulant now.

"Well, I mean to say, most people don't expect to live much beyond eighty. Shit! I certainly don't. So it seems fair to call forty middle-aged." She took another peppermint, frowned—reflective—before putting it in her mouth. "Funny," she said, "I can't imagine Bettina as a mother."

Johnny said, "I can't imagine *you* as one."

Delia, resting on one elbow, became motionless. Even her jaws stopped moving. Johnny stood up. He pulled off his T-shirt. "I'm going to have another little dip," he said. Then, "Care to join me?" he asked politely.

"What? Oh, no thanks. I'll wait till after lunch."

Johnny took his towel from the rail. He picked up his black bag, and went down the steps to the beach.

Delia reared into a sitting position. She covered her face with her hands, then ran them back over her hair. She breathed in, then let out the breath in three slow exhalations. She clambered up, and went over to the terrace rail. She looked at the sea, and then at the three rocks. "Gorgons, Furies, Fates," she said aloud. She turned, and headed for the house. Under the vine, pausing by the table, she lifted the champagne bottle from its bucket. She held it up to the light. It was about a quarter full. She put it back in the bucket, and went indoors.

Several minutes later, she emerged. In her right hand was a chunk of bread; buttered, and spread with a thick layer of amber chutney. In her left hand she held a slice of cold beef, which had been dipped in a red sauce. Some of this sauce dripped on to the tiled floor. She rubbed at it with her bare foot, partly obliterating the stain. Eating fast, she took alternate bites of beef and bread. Both were finished by the time she reached her mattress. She licked her fingers, and then wiped them on her hips.

Flopping on to the mattress, she sighed. She picked up the book about Piers, grimaced at it, and put it down. Next she took a pamphlet out of her basket, opening it at a page marked by a turned-down corner. She read two pages. Then she picked up a ballpoint pen and underlined a passage. She read on until, just after turning another page, she closed the pamphlet, stuffed it back into her basket, and rubbed her hand across her forehead.

Now she stood up again. She stretched, and strolled into the shade of the vine. She stopped by the drinks trolley. She picked up a bottle of brandy. Holding its neck in her right hand—her gaze was fixed on the words Rémy Martin—she gently stroked its side with her left hand before putting it back on the trolley. Next she picked up a bottle of pale vermouth. She was studying the intricate blue pattern on its label when a sound made her turn her head. Johnny, watching her, stood at the top of the terrace steps.

She nearly dropped the bottle, but, clutching it with both hands, saved it. Over her face and neck raced a frantic redness; it was shades deeper than the flush with which she had responded to Johnny's question about "picking".

"Why, Delia, you look as if I'd caught you *in flagrante delicto*."

"You startled me." She put the vermouth bottle back on the trolley without looking at it; it clinked loudly against another bottle, and she winced.

"What a nervous girl you are!"

"Shit! I'm not a girl. I'm a woman," she said, turning her back on the trolley.

"Woman, then. Really, you liberated ladies are so strange! I'd love people to call me that—a boy, I mean."

"Not much danger of that, these days, Johnny."

He put up a hand to the muscle at the corner of his mouth. Then he said, "Just a quick shower." He hung his towel over the terrace rail, and picked up his T-shirt from the stretcher. Carrying T-shirt and bag, he went past Delia into the house.

At once she emerged from the shade, and went over to the mattress. Stooping, she picked up a packet of chewing-gum. She tore off its wrapping, which she dropped on the mattress. Then she put all six little sugared rectangles in her mouth. Jaws rotating, she wandered to the centre of the rail, and looked towards the rocks. Grasping the rail, she ran her hands along it, together and farther and farther apart till her right hand touched Johnny's towel, and she grabbed it, and hurled it down onto the beach. For a moment, she hesitated. Then she returned to the mattress. Now she sat upright. She pulled the pamphlet out of her basket, and opened it at random. She stared at the page in front of her, but her eyes did not move.

Johnny came out of the house, carrying his bag. She looked up as he put it down next to the table under the vine. He wore his *Ganglion* T-shirt, with trunks striped in two shades of blue.

"I would have put on some music," he said, "but there's nothing except Mozart. You'd think there'd be *something* else. Bettina used to have all sorts of tapes and records. Now there's just this *plethora* of Mozart."

"I don't mind Mozart," said Delia.

"Noël Coward said Mozart was like piddling on flannel," Johnny said. He laughed.

"Shit! *Noël Coward* would!" Then she said, "I've never known anyone with so many pairs of swimming-trunks as you."

"That's because I'm a *beachcomber*, Delia. Beachcombers need lots of beach clothes. A remittance man—ah, if only there were more to remit! God, I'm thirsty. D'you find that swimming makes you thirsty? Or perhaps it was the champagne. And it's really very hot. Why don't we sit in the shade for a bit?" He gestured towards the pine table.

She frowned, rubbing the back of her hand across her forehead. It came away soaked, and sweat was trickling down between her breasts. "Yeah, perhaps I will," she said. "Just for a little. Though it seems a waste of my precious ten days' sunshine."

"Can't you stay a bit longer?"

"Not possibly. There's the AGM at the end of the month, and—oh so many other things. I feel guilty to be here at all, but it's been so long since I took a holiday. Shit!—three years, apart from the odd day or two added onto a weekend."

"For a binge?" he asked in a tone of polite interest.

She looked startled. "Well," she said, "all that's over now." She paused. "Bettina seemed so particularly keen for me to come."

"She's irresistible," he said.

Delia nodded. "Yeah."

Johnny was collecting used glasses and ashtrays. He put them with the champagne cooler, on the tray; he took the tray indoors. After a minute or two, he emerged with clean ashtrays, which he redistributed; one of them he put on the table under the vine. He went over to the drinks trolley and fetched tissues, from a box on its lower shelf, to wipe the surface of the table. He screwed up the used tissues, and dropped them in a straw waste-paper basket that stood behind the trolley. Delia, sitting on her mattress, chewing gum, observed him. Now, picking up the bottle of Perrier, he asked, "Anything for you, Delia?"

"Not right now."

His own drink completed—Perrier, decked with ice and lemon—he brought it to the table. "Come on lazybones. Get moving!" he said, in a pleasant tone, to Delia. He went towards his stretcher. Near it, he halted, frowning. "My towel!" he said, and looked all round. Then he walked to the terrace rail, and peered over. "There it is! But how extraordinary, when there's not a breath of wind." He shrugged, and went down the steps to the beach.

Delia, a smile on her face, stood up. She moved to the table under the vine, and pulled out a chair, opposite the one in front of which Johnny had put his Perrier. She sat down. Tilting the chair on to its back legs, she rocked.

Johnny reappeared at the top of the steps. He hung his towel over the rail again, arranging it with care, so that its edges were precisely aligned. Then he collected his cigarettes and lighter from the table beside the stretcher. Meanwhile, Delia had stopped rocking. As he approached the table, she said, "Oh, I'll have a glass of that Perrier, after all. Just like yours, in one of those tall glasses."

He put his cigarettes and lighter down on the table, next to his glass, and went to the trolley. While he was preparing her drink. Delia leant forward and picked up his scratched and battered lighter. She was fingering it when he came back, put her Perrier in front of her, and sat down.

She replaced the lighter on the table. "That's a funny lighter," she said. "For you, I mean. I'd have thought

66

you'd have something frafly Cartier-fartier, doncher know."

"A friend gave it to me. A great friend. An American. He's dead now."

At the word "American", Delia's nostrils had twitched. Now she said, "Oh, I'm sorry."

"He was awfully badly wounded in Vietnam. Never recovered."

At "Vietnam", Delia had grimaced outright. However, all she said was, "That dreadful war!"

"Probably just as well he died. He could never have borne life as a cripple. He'd been very athletic." Johnny paused. "We used to ski together."

"Ski!" said Delia. "Shit!—I'd hate to ski. I can't stand mountains."

"I simply love them."

"So big and heavy and grand. Looming over you."

"Rather noble, mountains."

"And so cold."

"The cold's awfully exhilarating."

"Yuck," said Delia. Then, "It's the sea I like. Warm sea of course—not that icy water round Britain. Shit!—I wouldn't go into that if you paid me. This Mediterranean's just about OK, but the Indian Ocean's my ideal."

"Like swimming in hot soup. I think the sea's rather boring."

"Yet you swim a lot."

"That's just healthy exercise."

"Health again!" Delia laughed. She removed the chewing-gum from her mouth, rolled it between her fingers, then put it in Johnny's ashtray. When he winced, she laughed again, picked it up, and stuck it to the underside of the table.

"Really, Delia!"

She took a drink of Perrier—about half the glassful —then rested her elbows on the table, and cupped her chin in her hands. "You know, Johnny, I think you and I feel the opposite about everything in the world. Every single thing. Hot and cold. Sea and mountains. Etcetera, etcetera, etcetera."

Johnny laughed. He said, "We could turn it into a game."

"A game?"

"Yes. You say hot and I say cold. And so on. A sort of truth game."

"If we're going to play a truth game, you must take off those dark glasses, man. I like to see a person's eyes."

"Must I? Oh, all right." Johnny took off his sunglasses, and put them down on the table. He blinked his eyes: they were grey-blue; the irises seemed very large.

"That's better! So I say hot."

"And I say cold."

"And I say sea."

"And I say mountains."

There was a pause. Then Johnny smiled. He said, "Arabs."

"Jews," said Delia. Then she added, "I don't mean *Israelis*, though."

"This game has one rule," said Johnny. "Straight answers. No qualifications. OK?"

"OK."

Johnny said, "True blue."

"Deepest red. 'The colour of life itself,' as Gorki said."

"Did he? What on earth did he mean?"

"Oh, he was talking about blood. I think it was a scene of childbirth. . . ."

"How very unpleasant. Turks."

"Greeks," said Delia. "Though of course I don't believe in national stereotypes."

"No qualifications!"

"Shit! Still it's only a game."

"Dogs."

"Cats." She paused, then said, "It's strange, that. You'd think it would be the other way round."

"Why?"

"Oh, I don't know."

"I find doggy devotion rather touching. Loyal chaps and all that."

"Yeah," said Delia, "and they're upper-class. All those upper-class people dote on their doggies." She said, "Cats are independent." Then, "It's funny. I've never known Bettina without a cat before."

"It's true. She's always had a cat."

"Yeah. In Durban it was a Siamese."

"Was it? I say America! Good old Uncle Sam!"

"Greed plus God. I say Mother Russia."

"Snow and salt-mines. Do you *really* mean it? Modern Russia?"

"In Tsarist days, there was some princess whose coach-man froze to death while she was at a party. And when they told her, she said, "But how shall I get home?""

Johnny laughed. He said, "But seriously, Delia, if you had to choose, would you really live in Russia rather than America?"

Delia hesitated. She said, "Of course, there's the language problem. I'm not much of a linguist."

"And you've got used to freedom."

"Freedom! To live in ghettos with rats and pimps and drug-pushers. Twenty million Americans go to bed hungry. And all those guns and murders. In the Soviet Union, at least one can walk the streets at night."

"I never knew that was your ambition."

"What do you mean?"

"To walk the streets at night. In the snow, too."

"Oh, shit, man!" But, reluctantly, she smiled.

"I say, North."

"South. Except in London. I could never live in farty-tarty SW something."

"I couldn't live anywhere else. I say Right."

"Isn't that the same as true blue? Left, of course."

"Europe."

"Africa."

He said, "White."

"Black. Well, I suppose, being white myself I can't say that. But in terms of South Africa. . . ."

"No qualifications."

"Black, then." There was a moment's pause. Delia said, "Women."

Johnny hesitated. Then he said, "Men."

There was another pause. Then Delia said, "It's funny. That friend of Bettina's, Micky van Rooyen. I never knew they were so close. That deathbed scene and everything. Bettina's a mysterious person in some ways."

Johnny said, "Bettina bloweth where she listeth."

"Hunh?"

"She's like the wind. It's something I remember from Scripture, at school. 'The wind bloweth where it listeth.' It blows as it chooses. You hear the sound of it, but you can't tell where it came from or where it's going. That's Bettina."

Delia said, "That walk of hers. Like people in Botticelli's pictures. Shit! Angels and goddesses, and so on.

Their feet hardly seem to touch the ground." Then, "That's what she was saying this morning about those maenads."

"It's because she puts her weight on the balls of her feet, never on her heels." He paused. "I adore her."

Delia said, "You always talk in an exaggerated way. But when you said that, you really sounded quite sincere."

"Oh, how perfectly awful. I do apologize." He took a sip of Perrier. Delia had finished hers.

"No need to apologize, Johnny."

"I can't stand sincerity. There's only one thing worse, and that's *frankness*." He lit a cigarette.

"I admire them both."

"Here we go again. But, actually, Delia—frankly, as *you* might say—don't you get fed up with being so sincere all the time? So dedicated to *the cause*? Doesn't it get awfully monotonous?"

She felt under the table for the chewing-gum she had stuck there, pulled it off, started to mould the grey-pink lump between her fingers. She looked up. She said, "You know, this is the first time since I've been here that our eyes have met. Even when you're not wearing those dreadful glasses, we seem to avoid meeting each other's eyes."

"*Their eyes met at last!*" Johnny placed his hand over his heart.

"Oh, shit! Johnny, you're so fucking frivolous."

"That's awfully unfair. I asked you a perfectly serious question, and you avoided answering it."

"No, I didn't. The other thing just happened to strike me. About our eyes."

He said, "All those meetings. Those minutes of meetings. Those endless committees."

". . . *the flat ephemeral pamphlet and the boring meeting.*"

71

"So you *do* feel it!"

"Sorry to disappoint you. That's not me. It's W. H. Auden."

"Oh, Auden. I had a friend who was very keen on Auden. He told me Auden used to talk about 'Miss God'." Johnny laughed.

Delia said, "They're *necessary*, Johnny. Meetings and pamphlets. They get things done."

"Even when you have to work with all those inefficient blacks?"

"Not so inefficient, Johnny. They're fighting a war. They're going to make a revolution."

"And you support them?"

"Yeah! All the way!"

"And you believe they'll win?"

"Yeah, I do."

"And you believe that one day you'll go back?"

"Back home? Oh, *yes*."

Johnny leant back in his chair. He inhaled smoke, blew it out. He said, "The country's changed a lot, you know. I wonder if you'd recognize Durban. So many new roads. Freeways."

"Yeah, I've heard. They've put big new roads everywhere. To make things easy for the police and the army."

Johnny looked surprised. He said, "I suppose that is one reason." He paused, then said, "And you'd find new slabs of concrete looming everywhere."

"Yeah, I've heard. I had a couple of friends. You wouldn't have known them. They rented a shack on the coast—near Elephant Rock. I used to love to go there. It was right on the edge of the sea. Just below was a rock pool—the walls were crusted with layers of old shells. There was coral, too, and weed that was so green it shocked you. Little fish darted about. Shit!—they looked *diaphanous*. And the water was so clear. Yet, at night, it felt like velvet."

Johnny shivered. He stubbed out his cigarette. "Ugh," he said. "I can't bear swimming at night."

"I love it! Anyway, I heard that now there are big villas all along that coast. And a big block of flats where the shack used to be. Holiday flats, of course—it isn't even as if they were flats for the workers."

"Would they be more attractive if they were?"

"Oh, shut up, man." But she smiled. Then she said, "Of course, my friends had given up the shack long ago. He's in jail for fifteen years, and she's banned and not allowed out of Durban. But, what I was going to say is that, for me, that shack's still there. The shack, and that stretch of coast with no other buildings, and the rock pool. Velvety at night and transparent in the day time. Nothing's changed. It's all safe in my head. Preserved like big golden plums in brandy."

Johnny said, "Do you realize what you're saying? When you go back—*if* you go back—you won't be able to preserve that old South Africa of yours in your head any more. In brandy."

Delia looked blank for an instant. Then she said, "I'll be able to face up to that when the time comes. It'll be worth it, then."

"Because the workers will be able to move into the holiday flats? But, seriously, Delia, do you really look forward to living in a black South Africa?"

"It won't be *black*. It will be non-racial."

"Rubbish! You'll be bossed about by the blacks."

"That's not how I see it."

"But that's how it's going to be."

"We'll all be working together for a socialist society, not a black one."

"Rubbish! You'll be a dog's-body, just as you are now, for people who haven't a tenth of your brains, or drive, or character."

"Shit! You really believe that, don't you? That blacks are stupider and lazier than whites. That they're *nastier*. You believe it even though you know what white South Africa's like. Bone-headed. Blinded by colour. And the 'white supervisor' asleep in the van while the Africans do the work. And the torture and the massacres. The *evil*. Surely you can see what's in front of your eyes, man?"

But Johnny's eyes were wandering. He shrugged. "Oh, well. Anyway, I can't really get worked up about it. My only links to the place are my mama and my teeny bit of money. Otherwise, I couldn't care less."

"Shit, Johnny—that country *made* you. It's part of you. It's like denying yourself when you deny your country."

"I don't think of it as *my* country."

"You don't? What is *your* country, then? England?"

He hesitated. "I suppose so."

"*Really*? Oh, Johnny, you amaze me. Whatever problems we'll have to face, building the new South Africa —don't make that snooty face, man—I can always cheer myself up when I think of the alternative. Staying in England."

"You hate the climate?"

"Well, there's that, of course. The cold, the damp, the greyness. Even in summer, when you've had two fine days, there's a storm, and then it's cold and grey again. But it's not just the climate. There's the countryside. Shit! Those awful silent villages. Not just in the Cotswolds. All of them. Like cemeteries. I know they usedn't to be, once, but they are now. Silent, and spick and span. The real country people can't afford to live in them. The cottages have all been bought by retired types and weekenders. Tories to a man, and busy with their bloody gardens. No one to talk to. And outside the villages, it's dreadful. Especially in winter. Those horrible bare trees that look as if they're quite dead, and the dead earth, and the dead grey sky. And seeing one's breath steaming in the air, like a dragon's. Shit! It's a bit better in summer, I suppose, with the trees fluffed up green, like candy floss! But—yuck! —how *insipid*!"

Johnny was laughing. "Oh, Delia, what a lot you miss. Those beautiful houses in their great landscaped parks."

"Yes, well, those houses are museums, really, aren't they, even if old, titled people still live in some of them? Not people I'd ever want to meet, though. All those dogs, and that horse-riding, chasing after poor foxes."

"Oh, Delia, *not* horse-riding: *riding*. What can one ride except a horse?"

Delia said, "A bike."

Johnny shrugged. He said, "Presumably you don't find London *quite* as awful as you find the country?"

"London? Well, when I first got there I thought it was hideous."

"Oh, Delia! The architecture, the history. . . ."

"Yeah, well, it took me some time to notice all that. At first it just seemed so dingy and dreary and cramped. Those dark-brick houses glued together, with no space in between. Shit!—and all those basements with dirty net curtains. But after a bit I did begin to look at it differently. The great city, you know. People of all kinds and colours. Black kids talking with cockney accents. The public parks. Art galleries, theatres, concerts—though I hardly ever seem to go to them. Wonderful bookshops. Interesting programmes on television—though of course the Tories are going to change that. They're really longing to kill the BBC. Tories hate anything that makes people think, anything that's uncommercial. Oh shit, the whole place is getting so rotten with callousness and greed. Worse and worse all the time. Soon, it'll be as bad as New York. More and more violence by desperate people. People with no hope, no beliefs, no future. Posh parts and ghettos. Wherever there are decent houses, they push the poor people out, and *gentrify*."

"Poor people? Nobody's poor in England."

"Not stark starving poor like they are back home. But, all the same, there's real poverty in England. Degradation and homelessness—more and more people sleeping in the streets—and hopelessness. And it looks so squalid in that cold grey light. While the rich are getting richer all the time. And they're such swines."

"Swine, you mean."

"Swine or swines—that's what they are. Mad about money. Spending fortunes on clothes and in smarty-tarty restaurants. Staying in the hotels that lots of those great country houses of yours have been turned into, where they pay and pay to be treated as if they're important, when they're *nothing*. Revelling in the respect their money gets them, and the luxury, and the posh atmosphere. Frafly, frafly culchahed, doncher know! Yeah, they like a nice little touch of culchah! They love to say they've seen that fucking garden at Sissinghurst. And then there's Glyndebourne—simply supah! But—shit!—they don't care a stuff about the music, just about dressing up, and showing off their pricey picnics." She paused for breath. "Anyway," she said, "all those things are only by-products. Of the money madness. *The scum rises to the top*. I've always said that. What one's got to do is skim it off"—she made a sweeping gesture—"and chuck it out with the garbage."

Delia was panting. Johnny, smiling, was leaning back in his chair. He said, "And I feel exactly the opposite. The dregs sink to the bottom, and all one can do is *leave* them there."

"Yuck! That's revolting. But it's no use our arguing." She paused. "Funny, though," she said, "I've never felt we were *quite* so far apart as when you said that England was your home."

"I didn't say precisely that. I don't entirely feel it. Perhaps I'm really a man without a country. A beachcomber, as I said before. Home's rather a repulsive idea, in any case. Cosy, but menacing. Like a very soft, thick pillow. You can sink into it, but someone may pull it out from under your head, and suffocate you with it."

"What a weird idea! Shit!—that's not at all how I feel. I feel *homesick*."

"But you believe you'll go home—eventually?"

"Yeah."

"And that will make everything worth while?"

"Yeah."

"Then, Delia, you should be gloriously happy. Are you gloriously happy?"

Delia slumped forward, resting her weight on her left elbow. She still circled the chewing-gum between the thumb and first two fingers of her right hand. "Well, of course," she said, "this is a very stressful time in our history."

"But the good and the true will triumph. You believe that?"

"Yes!"

"*I* think you're troubled by doubts."

"No!"

"I really think so. That's why you've got this drinking problem you were talking about."

"Shit! It's *not*. It's just the stress that causes that."

Johnny leant forward slightly. "Then why aren't you having a drink or two here? Surely this is a break from all that stress? Your first holiday in three years, didn't you say? Just ten precious days, and this is the third. *I* think you should relax completely. A drink or two would relax you. I can see you aren't relaxed, from the way you fidget all the time."

Delia said, "You're very observant, all of a sudden. I never thought you noticed what I did."

"Of course I notice." He leant farther forward. There was a long encounter between eyes, this time. He said, "After all, we're old friends."

Her expression became hard. She looked away. "Old friends!" she said. "Shit! I remember you talking to me about being friends once before. Do *you* remember? I was desperate for money, and I telephoned to ask you if you could lend me a bit. Bettina was away somewhere. I couldn't get hold of her, and I couldn't think of anyone else to ask. None of my friends have money. So I asked you. I felt sure you could have lent it to me. But you said no."

"I can hardly remember. . . ."

"It wasn't so much your not lending me the money that I minded. I said, 'Sorry to have bothered you, Johnny.' And you said, 'Nonsense, Delia. That's what friends are for.' I thought it was like the kiss of Judas, your saying that, when I felt sure you could have lent me the money."

"You're wrong. Of course I would have lent you the money if I'd had it. I can remember now. I was very short indeed. I'd lost a job. I hadn't been well. I suppose I should have gone and borrowed the money for you from someone else, but I didn't realize how desperate you were and—I hadn't been well. But I promise you're wrong, Delia. You know, just because I make a lot of silly jokes, it doesn't mean I'm a liar or that I don't *feel* things."

"Shit! Surely, Johnny, you're not claiming to be *sincere*? As you were just saying, that's almost as bad as being *frank*."

He lowered his head for a moment, gazed down at the table. When he looked up, tears were oozing from his eyes.

"Shit! Oh, Johnny, man! Hell, I'm sorry." Delia transferred the lump of chewing-gum to her left hand, then stretched out her right hand and touched his arm, which jerked. "Johnny. Cheer up. Johnny, I believe you. *Really*."

"You do?" he said, lowering his head, and dabbing at his eyes with his fingers. "Really?" He leant back, and she took away her hand. He wiped the fingers of both hands across his eyes in an outward movement. Then he smiled. "Oh, I'm so glad. I feel quite different. As if a cloud between us had suddenly blown away."

Delia said, "I always thought you didn't like me."

"Silly girl—woman, I mean. Sorry!"

Delia smiled.

Johnny blinked. "Whew," he said, and then, "I feel like a drink. A glass of champagne. But I can't drink champagne alone. Come on, Delia. Join me. To celebrate."

She said, "Apart from anything else, I gave up for my health. I want to go back to England feeling really fit."

"So you shall. A glass of champagne can't do you any harm. Champagne's actually *good* for you. I remember once, when my mama was convalescing from an operation, the doctor *prescribed* champagne. 'A glass of champagne every morning at eleven.' That was what he said."

"Shit!—you're joking, man."

"No, I'm not. It *is* a tonic. It raises your spirits—as well as being so delicious. I'll open a fresh bottle. Bettina's drinks-fridge is full of the stuff—and all of it the very best, of course. Come on, Delia. Let's celebrate."

There was a silence. Then, "Oh, well," she said. "After all, I am on holiday. And you say it's a tonic. And we've got something to celebrate." She paused. Then she said, "Shit—*champagne*! But just one glass."

Now she rested her forehead on her right hand, and looked down at the table. Johnny sprang up. No twitch or pulse spoilt his face. Even time's natural lines seemed charmed away. He was transfigured by exultancy: he shone.

She said, "Put on a bit of that Mozart, hey?"

"OK." He picked up his dark glasses, and put them on. Then, bag in hand, he strode into the house.

Delia continued to gaze at the table. She was still moulding her lump of chewing-gum between her fingers. She looked up when she heard the first bars of the Twentieth Piano Concerto in D minor; sombre, restless, unnerving. Thirty seconds later, she stood up. The pressure of the music increased, and she ran into the house. The music's threat was manifest; then the sound was severed.

A few moments later, she came back onto the terrace. She ambled towards the rail and looked towards the rocks. "Shit!" she exclaimed, and hurled her chewing-gum down onto the beach. Then she turned round, and hurried back into the shelter of the vine. She dumped herself in her chair. It screeched on the tiles, as she jerked it close to the table.

AFTERNOON

At the table under the vine, Bettina, her back to the house, faced the sea. Delia sat on her right, Johnny on her left.

Bettina winced. She said, "It's hard to imagine that all this actually looked quite *pretty* an hour ago."

She was clearing away the debris of their lunch. Just behind her stood a trolley. On its lower shelf were two empty wine bottles and the used plates and cutlery she had already put there. Now she began to transfer serving-dishes on which the remains of food were drying up or melting. Slices of pink flesh had shrivelled. Glaze slid from mud-coloured pâté in the narrow coffin of a terrine. Mould-green sauce, dissolving, exposed a chicken's severed thigh, and a few jaundiced potatoes seemed to sweat their dressing. Brown, mucous lettuce leaves clung to the sides of a salad bowl; at the bottom, one green bean lay curled like a worm.

"Shit! It was simply great." Delia, high-coloured, sprawled in her chair. There was a grease-stain on the left breast of her bathing-dress.

Johnny, opposite, lounged with grace. His white *Ganglion* T-shirt was still perfectly fresh. He was wearing his dark glasses. "Delicious!" he said to Bettina. "And it did look awfully pretty. But, darling, you hardly ate a thing."

"I wasn't very hungry." Bettina put the pâté on the upper shelf of the trolley. Her hair was smooth, her face

pale and matt. Apart from its colour—lilac—her kaftan
was identical to the one she had worn that morning.

"A lettuce leaf, a few French beans?" Johnny, head
cocked, was quizzical.

"I seem to have gone off meat." A fly buzzed. Johnny
started, as, sudden as a cat, Bettina struck at it; her hand,
the fingers curved together, was a white paw with silver
claws. The fly vanished, and Bettina picked up the dish of
potatoes. Delia stretched out, and took one. As she carried
it to her mouth, oil dripped on to the pink linen tablecloth,
and she said, "Oops! Sorry!"

Bettina said, "That's all right. But I'm afraid I took
away your plate too soon. I could give you another?"

Delia shook her head, mouth busy with potato. When
she had swallowed it, she said, "Shit, no. I've had quite
enough. That was just a sudden compulsion. I've always
loved eating with my hands."

Johnny said, "Ugh! I loathe having greasy fingers."

Delia was licking hers. She shook her head. She said,
"But it's so nice to *feel* the food. Forks are just barriers. I
can never understand why they were invented. As for
cake-forks. . . ."

Johnny said, "Oh, well, I agree with you about *cake-*
forks. Awfully middle-class."

"Yeah," said Delia. "My mom had them. But I don't
like any kind of fork. Knives are all right. You have to cut
things, sometimes. And I suppose you need spoons for
sweets."

"Puddings, you mean?" said Johnny.

"Yeah, if you call things like ice-cream and stewed fruit
'puddings'."

"I do," said Johnny.

Delia giggled. "*I do,*" she repeated. "You sound as if

86

you're getting married." Then, "I can't understand why you call those things 'puddings'."

Johnny said, "No, I suppose you can't."

Bettina said, "Now, one can't tell which part of the terrace is in the sun and which in shadow. The sky's quite white."

"But it's still just as hot," said Johnny.

Bettina said, "The air's absolutely still, and so's the sea."

Delia giggled again. She said, "Shit! I suppose it's *posh* to call sweets 'puddings'."

Johnny said, "What about soup, Delia? Surely even you need a spoon for that."

"One can drink it, or sop it up with bread. Not at smarty-tarty dinner parties of course." She paused. Then, "When I'm alone, I usually eat with my hands."

Johnny said, "*Boeuf à la bourguignonne?*" He laughed.

"Beef stew? I never seem to make stew. Not having a kitchen of my own. Anyway, I don't get the time. But, if I did—" She hesitated. Then, "I have Indian friends who eat all sorts of things with their fingers. I love it when I go to their place."

Bettina said, "Indians eat with such delicacy. Only using one hand. They manipulate the food so elegantly that their fingers never get greasy."

Tilting her head far back, Delia swallowed the last drops of wine in her glass. Then she picked up the bottle that stood in the middle of the table. She poured nearly all that was left in it into her glass. She raised the bottle in the air. "Who's for vino?" she asked.

Bettina said, "No more for me."

Johnny said, "I've still got some."

Delia poured the remaining wine—except a few drops that spilled on the tablecloth—into her own glass. It was now full to the brim. Putting the empty bottle down on the table, she smiled at Bettina. "Are we going to have some more of this?" she asked. Then, "It's really refreshing, isn't it?"

Bettina said, "I find that a lot of wine in the middle of the day makes me hot. But of course we'll open another bottle, if you want some more." Now she put the empty bottle and her own glass on the trolley. Johnny and Delia were holding their glasses, and there was nothing on the table but the stained cloth, at which Bettina glanced with distaste. Standing up, she pulled it off with a deft flick.

"Bettina, the matador," said Johnny. "*Olé!*"

Delia said, "Shit! How I hate the very idea of bullfights."

Johnny's face brightened. "When I was last in Spain," he began—but Bettina was turning to push the trolley into the house, and he broke off. "Let me do that," he said.

"No, really," said Bettina.

"*Really* really?"

"*Really* really. If I wanted you to do it, you know I'd let you. Just as I let you drive into town and do the shopping for me yesterday. But I feel like doing this. I'm filled with a blessed rage for order. I shall deal ruthlessly with all the leftovers and fill the dishwasher to the brim."

"OK, then," said Johnny.

Delia said loudly, "Isn't there something *I* can do?"

Bettina said, "No, not a thing. In a few minutes, I'll bring out some fruit and some Turkish coffee."

As Bettina started pushing the trolley away, Delia said, "And some wine."

Bettina, without turning round, said, "Right." She wheeled the trolley indoors.

Johnny felt under his chair, and brought out a clean

ashtray. His cigarettes and lighter were in it. He lit a cigarette.

Delia, looking out to sea, glass in hand, started to rock her chair backwards and forwards.

A minute passed. Then Johnny said, "Children are always told not to do that."

"Not to do what?"

"Not to rock their chairs like that."

Delia laughed. "But I'm no child! Shit!" A moment later, she stopped rocking. She turned towards Johnny, and said, "Funny you should mention children. It chimed with my thoughts. I was thinking about eating with my hands, as a child. Eating *putu*."

"*Putu*?" said Johnny.

"Shit, Johnny, man, you certainly have become English. Or perhaps you were always that way—up in the White Highlands. But surely you know what *putu* is? *Mielie pap*. Perhaps you don't understand that, either. Maize porridge, Fairfield, old chap. That stiff white porridge that's made from mealies."

Johnny grimaced. "That stuff the blacks eat?"

"Yeah. I suppose you've never tasted it. *That stuff the blacks eat*. Shit!—you're dead right, there, man! Just about all they do eat, often. Even in quite a prosperous house-hold, like my mom and dad's. Boys' meat once a week. *Boys' meat*—that's what you asked for at the butcher's. *Boys' meat*! God knows what it was. Mostly bones and gristle. And they had samp and beans. Have you ever tasted samp and beans?"

"Of course I've tasted *beans*."

"Tinned in tomato sauce?"

"More often in a *cassoulet*."

"Shit! Trust *you*! Is there anything you're not snobby

about? A class snob, a money snob, a food snob!" But Delia's tone and laugh were friendly.

Johnny's cigarette snapped just below the filter. He stubbed it out. He said, "I'm sure I've never tasted *samp*. I can't even remember what it is—if I ever knew."

"It's dried maize kernels, dried corn off the cob. You cook the samp and beans together. I used to love samp and beans. And I loved *putu*. Sometimes, when my parents were out, I'd sneak off to the maid's room. It was a little shed at the back of the house. Typical servants' quarters. Dark, with one tiny window high in the wall. Just like a cell. 'The girl's room,' my mom called it, though our maid was a woman of forty. Shit! *The girl's room!* 'The native *khaya*'—that's what my dad used to call it. He said to me, 'You're never to go into the native *khaya*.' Laying down the law as usual! That was part of the thrill, the joy of going there. To Septima's room."

Johnny laughed. "Septima! I've always been awfully amused by the *chic* names black women have. Septima, for instance, and Victoria and Charlotte and Lucy—while whites are usually called things like Sandra and Dawn and what they pronounce 'Di-Ann'." He said, "You were rather lucky to be called Delia."

"Yeah, I quite like it. It was my granny's name. My granny on my dad's side." Delia paused. "What was I saying? Oh yeah, I was telling you about Septima. She was so good to me. It must have been hell for her, leaving her own children—she had four, and her husband was dead —in the Transkei with her old mother. Having to work for us, and live in that shed, so as to earn money to send, to keep them alive. But she never took it out on me. Shit! Never! She was so gentle. I feel she knew my parents weren't fond of me, and tried to make up for it. And when my brother was born, and they were so fucking thrilled, she never let me feel neglected, or that she liked him better than me. Anyway, I don't think she did. Shit!—he was always a real whiner."

"I'd forgotten you have a brother."

"I've almost forgotten it, myself. He works in a bank. Married. I don't know what his wife's like, but she can't be much if she married him. Anyway—to hell with them. When I went to visit Septima in her room, we'd scoop up handfuls of *putu*, and dip them in a sauce. There was boys' meat in it, when she got her ration. Otherwise, she'd brew an onion, and perhaps a tomato, in water, with some curry powder. I believe it's only in Natal that the Africans make curry sauce—the Indian influence, you know. Curry's always been my favourite food. We never had it in our house—'coolie food', my dad called it. Anyway, when I think about it, I always think how kind of Septima it was, to share her food with me, with a greedy pig who had breakfast, dinner and tea. Shit!" Delia sighed. "I can remember the taste of that *putu* and curry sauce, now. And the smell of that little shed. Heavy, sweet, warm. *African*."

Johnny said, "*Le parfum africain*, my mother used to call it. A polite way of saying that they stank."

"*They*?"

"You know perfectly well who I mean. It's sheer affectation to pretend you don't. Just as it's sheer affectation to pretend they don't stink. But even if you admit that they do, I suppose you'll say that they can't afford deodorants."

"Shit! I *don't* admit it. But you're dead right they can't afford deodorants."

"Anyway, deodorants would only help a little bit. Their *basic* smell—everyone's got one, even if they *do* use deodorants—is so unpleasant." He grimaced.

"Unpleasant to *you*! Africans think *we* smell nasty. Sour, they say."

"My dear Delia, that's beside the point. I'm talking about *my* reactions."

"Yeah. You would be!" Delia gave a grunt of laughter. But then her thoughts seemed to move elsewhere: her forehead slightly wrinkled; her jaw sagged. Then, in a low tone, she said, "You know, Johnny, I wonder if why I remember that African food so clearly—as if I were eating it now—and why I feel it was so wonderful, is because, to me, it symbolizes . . . well . . . the only love I ever knew when I was a child."

Johnny said, "My God, how corny can you get!" He laughed. "Or perhaps I should say, how *mealy*!"

Suddenly Delia had the look of a nervous patient in the dentist's chair. She closed her eyes; she hunched her shoulders, and pressed the back of her head against them; she dug her elbows into her sides. Then she opened her eyes, and unlocked her body. She looked across the table at Johnny, and drank the wine in her glass. "Yeah," she said.

Although Bettina's step was so light, they both turned as she came out of the house. She carried a tray. On it, small lacquer-red cups held brown, frothy Turkish coffee; coldness fogged a wine bottle and glasses of water; on three thin amethyst plates lay silver fruit-knives. In a creamy bowl, little pale grapes clung together tightly, and there were figs: some a sleepy purple, others the fresh greens and yellows of caged birds.

As she put the tray down on the table, Johnny said, "Quite perfect, darling. A work of art!"

Bettina sighed. "Mmm," she said. Her crab pendant dangling, she stooped to hand round the coffee cups.

"There we are. Sweet for Delia, medium for me, and no sugar for Johnny."

Johnny said, "Surely that must *symbolize* something."

Bettina smiled. She said, "But *what*?" She put a glass of water next to each coffee cup, and sat down.

"Dear little grapes!" said Delia. Then she looked up, and pointed to the dark bunches overhead. "Pity *those* are so tasteless."

Bettina said, "Oh, you tried them?"

"Yes, just after I got here. I reached up and pulled one off, and ate it."

Bettina said, "You should have washed it."

Delia shrugged. "It looked so luscious. I was disappointed."

"Yes, those grapes are purely decorative, I'm afraid," said Bettina.

Delia said, "Can I have some wine?"

"Of course you may," said Bettina. She poured wine into the glass that Delia pushed towards her. Delia waited till it was full, then pulled it back and immediately took three large gulps.

"And now," said Bettina, "I'm going to have a cigarette." She smiled at Johnny, and he jumped up to fetch her packet of Disque Bleu from the table at which she had sat that morning.

As Johnny lit Bettina's cigarette, Delia said, "Your third today."

"That's right."

"Shit! You're amazing!" Delia paused. Then she said, "I was just thinking that I wish I could do everything beautifully, the way you do." She waved a hand over the things on the table.

Bettina said, "*Perfection of the life or of the work.*" Then she went on quickly, "It's just discipline. Habit. Like the way I smoke."

"But the trouble is," said Delia, "that I get so impatient. And it doesn't give me any real satisfaction. Shit! For instance, if I try to cook something elaborate, I always start wishing I was reading a good book instead."

"Very sensible," said Bettina. "I approve."

"And talking of good books," said Delia, "I didn't bring *one* with me. I was so certain there'd be plenty here. You've always bought all the good new novels and biographies, and so on. But that crappy book about Piers is the only novel I can find. Nothing but poetry and Greek plays, and books about the Ancient Greeks."

"I've been paring things down." Bettina smiled. "To the essentials."

Delia said, "Hell, I really love poetry. You know that. I'm just not quite in the mood for it yet."

Johnny said, "I nip into town and buy thrillers, from time to time. There's a tourist shop that has paperbacks. I can lend you something."

Delia said, "Shit! I don't want to read *rubbish*. As I said, I *love* poetry. It's just—"

Johnny said, "There was that poem of Professor Crowe's. Do you remember Crowe? A dried-up little man. Quite bald. He lectured on something fearfully dreary in the English department. I forget what. And I found this poem of his in an old magazine. I can still remember how it began. *Oft in my lusty boyhood, methought I was a peon of Peru.* That did rather captivate me."

Bettina laughed. Delia said, "It must have been an *awful blow* to you, Johnny, to have to come to varsity in Natal instead of going to Ox-fahd. You failed the entrance exam to Ox-fahd, didn't you?"

Several muscles moved in Johnny's face. He said, "My housemaster was quite certain I'd get in, but I had a sort of blackout, in one of the papers. Quite inexplicable."

Delia said, "Oh, *quite*. I wonder—"

Johnny said, "Poetry. We were talking about poetry. There's some sonnet of Shakespeare's about 'bare ruined choirs'. I believe he meant trees. But a friend of mine used to talk about 'bare ruined choirboys'. I thought that was rather funny."

Delia said, "Was that the same friend who told you about Auden saying 'Miss God'?"

"As a matter of fact, it was."

"Johnny's sole link with literature!" Delia turned to Bettina. "*You* know how I love poetry." She took another gulp of wine. "It's just that one has to concentrate. I haven't quite *unwound* yet after London. But, shit, I really love poetry." She finished the drink. "As a matter of fact, I wrote a poem myself recently."

"Not *true*!" said Johnny.

"Perfectly true, I assure you."

"Recite it, then."

"Shit, no. Don't think I'll do that."

"You've forgotten it."

"I have not."

"Bet you have!"

"I have not."

"Prove it."

"*Shit*! Why should I?"

Johnny shrugged and smiled. "You've forgotten it."

"I *haven't*." She reached for the bottle, filled her glass, gulped.

> *"White the night, with cold dry stars:*
> *Water dried in the well,*
> *Milk dried in the cow's udder,*
> *Maize dried in the starved cob."*

"Here come those mealies again," murmured Johnny, but Delia didn't hear.

> *"Speech dried in the people's mouths.*
> *Black men will come secretly in that white night."*

"*Come*? How exciting!" Johnny spoke at almost normal volume, and Bettina hissed, "Johnny, be quiet!"

> *"And, at morning, water will gush from the ground,*
> *Milk will glisten on the children's lips,*
> *Heads of maize will become a field of spears.*
> *And from silenced mouths will sound trilling of birds,*
> *Morning birds that signal an end to mourning,*
> *That summon black dawn after white night.*
> *Black the sky, with threat of storm, with promise of rain.*
> *After white night, black morning."*

Silence seemed long. Delia drank again, and then Johnny, who had looked preoccupied ever since Bettina told him to be quiet, stood up. Staying on the same spot, he moved his feet in a shuffling dance-step. He started to sing, to the tune of "The White Cliffs of Dover":

> *"There'll be blackbirds after*
> *The whites of Umtata,*
> *Tomorrow, just you wait and see.*
> *And, instead of maize and water,*
> *There'll be famine and slaughter,*
> *Tomorrow, when those blacks are free!"*

"Johnny!" said Bettina.

He didn't look at her. "Just a little thing I improvised recently," he said. "Now who can say I'm not *into* poetry?"

As he sat down, Delia stood up. "My swim," she said. "Think I'll have my swim. Just after lunch is the best time. I've always said so. I've always thought so."

Bettina said, "Your coffee. . . ."

"I'll have it when I come back."

"It'll be cold then."

"Oh, shit! All right." Picking up her coffee cup, she tilted it and her head back: too far, for grounds as well as coffee went into her mouth, and she grimaced and licked her lips. She put down her coffee cup, then, picking up her wine glass, drained it. Hands resting on the table, she pushed at her chair with the back of her thighs, then turned, and set off towards the steps to the beach. Reaching them, she swayed. She thrust out a hand, and grasped the rail. Carefully, she started down.

Bettina said to Johnny, "You were horrible. Perfectly horrible."

"Oh, darling. You know me. Incorrigibly frivolous!"

She disregarded the nervous charm of his smile, of his tone. "Horrible!" she repeated.

"Honestly, darling—that so-called poem of hers."

97

"You didn't give me a chance to tell her, but *I* found it rather moving."

"*Really?*"

"I hope she's all right. Go and have a look."

"Of course she's 'all right'." But he stood up, and strolled over to the rail. "Yes, she's plodding over the pebbles." He started to speak in the mode of a sports commentator. "Slightly unsteady perhaps, but on she goes. And she's got no towel with her, so I suppose she'll shake herself dry like a dog. And, yes, now she's reached the sea. And, yes, she's stepping into the water. And now she's striding out, splashing all the way. And now the water's up to those monumental thighs—yes, this a powerful contestant, very powerful. And now, yes, the water's over what she calls her waist. And on she ploughs. Now the water's over her bosom—plenty of that! And she ducks her head under—that should sober her up a bit! —and she's starting to swim. Yes, now she's swimming, swimming with big strong strokes. Plenty of *stamina* there." He turned. In his usual voice, he said, "She's perfectly OK," and strolled back across the terrace.

"Fool!" said Bettina as he sat down. Her smile was minimal: so small that it did not show her teeth; it merely stretched her lips a little.

With the forefinger of his right hand he touched her arm; it was a dab; he retracted his hand immediately. "Darling," he said, "I'm sorry. I suppose I was rather awful, but I find drunks so depressing." He paused. He said, "I suppose it's because of my father." Bettina's expression was softening, and he leant back in his chair. He said, "I suppose Delia's started on a *binge*. How awfully tedious *that* is going to be."

Bettina was frowning: to herself now, not at Johnny.

She circled her pendant gently between her fingers. Then she said, "I simply can't understand it. She was so determined. She wouldn't take a sip. Six months since she gave up. And then today, quite suddenly, before lunch. . . ." Bettina repeated, "I can't understand it."

Johnny said, "Drunks are like that." He said, "Apparently she hasn't got that *stamina* you were talking about this morning." He paused. Then, "I was there at the beginning—well, practically. I'd gone for a swim. And when I came back, there she was, swigging the remains of that champagne we'd had. Straight out of the bottle. Glug, glug, glug. I had a shower, and when I came back, she asked me to open some more." He shrugged. "What could I do? I couldn't refuse, could I?"

"No, of course not." Bettina sighed. "The decision's hers. She's a grown-up person. It's her life. This is her holiday."

"Yes. If she wants to spend it in a stupor, that's her affair. But it's rather boring for us." Smiling, he shrugged. "*Five days*, didn't she say these binges last?"

Bettina said, "It's *sad*." Then, "Just go and take another look, to make sure she's all right."

"Bettina, the benevolent!" He stood up and went over to the rail. "She's resting against one of those three rocks out there," he said. "The Furies. Head back, eyes closed. I wonder if she's dozed off. No, now she's raising her head." After a moment, he added, "She's starting to swim back. Yes, she's definitely quite OK."

"Ah," sighed Bettina. "Well, now we can stop worrying."

"*I* never started," said Johnny, returning to the table.

Bettina said, "Why do you dislike her so much?"

Johnny sat down. "Do I?"

"You know you do."

"Well, I admit I've never really understood what you see in her."

"You're being evasive."

He hesitated. Then, "Well, there is something coarse about her. You must admit she's rather *crude*, at times. That eternal 'Shit!', and eating with her hands, and so on."

"That's not all."

"There are those politics of hers," he said.

"I don't feel the same as you do about those."

"But you don't force your views down people's throats. And you're not a *Marxist*. Anyway, more and more of my chums are anti-apartheid. Why, it's quite fashionable these days. And I don't support those awful Boers—I think they're perfectly ghastly. But Delia's so monotonous about it. And so *righteous*. She deserted her own child —well, when she went in for sabotage, she must have known they were bound to be parted. Driving the car for those black pals of hers to blow up that installation. And she got away, and they're in jail for life. Yet she's *still* so goddamn aggressive. And *righteous*, as I said before. Does she feel a trace of guilt? Not our *Dee-dee*!"

"Oh, I wouldn't be too sure of that." Bettina took one of the amethyst-coloured plates and a fruit knife from the tray. She chose a green fig, and started to peel it. "Fruit?" she asked.

"No, thanks." Then, shaking his head, he said, "The *best* of us, indeed!"

Bettina was looking at him, head on one side—pensive —as Delia came up the steps.

Salty, sandy, Delia blazed. Water dripped from her serpent hair, and from her bathing-dress which, wet, had darkened to a richer red. "Shit! That was so great!" she gasped, pulling Johnny's towel from the rail. As, violently, she rubbed her head with it, he winced. Then she wound the towel round her, like a sarong, and ran her fingers down through her hair to tidy it a little, as she came towards the table. Her hip bumped against the chair with its back to the sea. "Who's it for?" she asked, dipping into the fruit bowl for a purple fig, biting straight into it with her strong teeth. "This fourth chair," she said. "Who's it for? Nobody ever sits in it."

Bettina had cut her peeled fig in half. She was studying the pink seeds bedded in its pale-green flesh. Now she looked up. "The fourth chair?" she said. Then she laughed. "Why, that's for the Commander."

"The *Commander*?" said Delia.

"Don't sound so alarmed. I'm not expecting visitors. Certainly not any naval officers." She laughed again. A trace of shrillness in the sound made Johnny glance at her, wrinkling his forehead. "I mean Mozart's Commander," she said. "The statue Don Giovanni asks to supper, and who accepts the invitation. The stone guest with the icy handshake."

"Who was he?" asked Delia.

"As I said, a statue. The statue of the father of a woman Don Giovanni had seduced. But you could also say that he was—Death." Bettina laughed again.

Delia said, "I don't know much about opera."

"You wouldn't, would you?" said Johnny. "You were proclaiming this morning how much you disapprove of Glyndebourne."

"Oh, that's because people go there to be posh, instead of for the music. Shit!—it isn't the *opera* I disapprove of."

Johnny said, "I would have expected you to think it *elitist*."

"Elitist? Shit!—you're certainly on the wrong track there, man. I hate that word. It really makes me puke." Finishing her fig, she swallowed the little stalk-like protrusion at its end. "Using *elitist* as an insult is just an excuse for depriving the people of their heritage."

Johnny raised his eyebrows. "Their heritage?"

"Yeah. Their cultural heritage. It isn't only the media that feed the workers pap. All sorts of people who call themselves left-wing encourage it by saying opera and Shakespeare and so on are elitist. Even good English is called elitist, for Christ's sake. I remember the *New Statesman* started a column called 'This English', quoting samples of the dreadful things people do to the language. Well, some of their crappy readers complained that it was *elitist*, so, of course they stopped it. Yuck! *Real* socialists want the workers to have the best. You name it—art, literature, opera. . . ."

"Soap opera's the only kind the *workers* want," said Johnny.

Delia stretched out her hand for the wine bottle, and filled her glass. She said, "I remember when I first came to England, there was still a little bit of decency around. There was still a government that wasn't actively against bringing art to the people."

"Oh, my God," said Johnny. "Art to the people!"

"Yeah. This lot just wants to turn them into zombies, singing along with the TV commercials. Shit! Anyway, in those days, there was this company called the Bubble Theatre that got a bit of government money. They were called that because they had this big plastic tent, shaped like a bubble. They'd set it up in a park, and put on shows for the local people. The seats cost practically nothing —they were free for kids and for pensioners. I remember going to see *The Beggar's Opera* when the Bubble was on Hackney Downs. It had been raining—as usual—and the ground was muddy. Although it was English so-called summer, it was cold. But the tent was packed with local people. Most of them had probably never been to a theatre before. And—shit!—they enjoyed it, really enjoyed it. They laughed and clapped and had a helluva good time."

Johnny said, "Were they professionals—these Bubble people?"

"Yeah. Just about."

Johnny said, "There's nothing I loathe more than amateur theatricals."

"Shit! Trust you! I always say that's one of the signs of a real pseud. Pseuds just go to see *stars*, and to say how mahvlus, simply mahvlus they were. I often find I think about the *words* more—the meaning—when the acting's not all that hot. With Shakespeare, for instance. Of course the play has got to be good. No point in going to see amateurs in a bad play. *Stars* are the only thing that makes a bad play bearable."

Bettina said, "I think it sounds splendid about *The Beggar's Opera*. Really splendid. But I wonder if that audience would have enjoyed *Don Giovanni*."

Delia said, "What I want to do is give them the chance to find out. And, if they don't enjoy it, they should have opportunities, lots of opportunities to learn how. But —shit!—a lot of these so-called 'Militants' don't feel that, at all. Why, I heard about a school where some of the teachers deliberately didn't teach the children. They said it was so as to stop them participating in a corrupt society. Shit! And it was called William Tyndale, that school. There's a sick joke for you. Tyndale was the man who brought the Bible to the people, to stop it just being a secret book for Roman Catholic priests. Tyndale translated the New Testament, and smuggled it into England, and he was killed for it. They strangled and burnt him. The Roman Church was determined that ordinary people shouldn't read the Bible, in case they started to think for themselves. The Church wanted to go on feeding them mumbo-jumbo and hocus-pocus. There were all these 'Mysteries'—shit!—and they wanted to keep people mystified. But Tyndale said that he wanted to bring the Bible to every ploughboy."

Johnny said, "You amaze me, Delia. Propagating religion?"

"Shit! I'm not doing that. Of course I'm not. But at least the Reformation was an improvement on what went before it."

Bettina said, "Except that they got rid of the goddess."

Delia said, "The goddess?"

"Yes. The goddess Mary. Of course she's a goddess. Born sinless and never sinning. Mating with the old god and giving birth to the young one, yet remaining a virgin. Even taken up physically into heaven—wherever 'up' is. The Roman Catholics and the Eastern Church had the sense to keep the goddess. Of course, they say that they pray 'through' her, not 'to' her. But it isn't true. Women pray 'to' her. The living goddess. On this island, peasant women actually leave food under her icon."

"How awfully sweet," said Johnny.

"Much more than that," said Bettina. "Go into a Protestant church—Methodist, Lutheran, Church of England, or whatever you like—and you'll always feel the chill. The small ones are like village halls or damp deserted little vaults. The large ones are like museums or public assembly-rooms. Look at St Paul's—a great big beautiful municipal building. The goddess has been banished, and she has taken her revenge. Of course, the Judaic tradition in Christianity always fought her. Judaism, like Islam, has such a deadening maleness."

Johnny said, "Darling, it all sounds most impressive."

Delia said, "Well—shit!—of course I disapprove of male domination. But, Bettina, surely you prefer the Renaissance to the Middle Ages?"

Bettina leant back. She smiled. "Mmm. Classical light pouring into that cobwebby world—the true illumination, as far as I'm concerned." She sighed. "But there's always a Savonarola lurking in the cellar. Waiting to pounce out and spoil things. To make Botticelli paint those endless madonnas and children instead of Aphrodite and Chloris."

Delia said, "Did you know they did a survey in England that showed that the 'Top People' are the ones that go to church most. Shit! Just what I would have expected. What all religion stands for is keeping things the way they are: the Top People on top and the workers at the bottom."

Johnny yawned. "Do I remember some phrase about the opium of the people?"

Delia said, "Opiate, not opium. Perfectly true, of course. Anyway, one good thing is that working-class people believe in religion less and less. In northern countries they hardly go to church at all. Even in Mediterranean countries, only the old people go, except at Easter and Christmas. And I'm glad, glad, glad." She struck the table with her fist.

Bettina said, "What do they do instead?"

Delia said, "Oh, all sorts of things. Anyway, at least

they don't go to church. Down with Christianity!" Again she struck the table.

Johnny said, "What about Islam?"

Delia shuddered. "The Muslims are a real menace. Creeping over Africa now. Shit! Far worse than the Christians—though I can't stand them either. Yuck! When I think of my dad! And my mom, going along with him." She turned to Bettina. "Was your mother religious?"

"Only just enough to mind my marrying a Jew."

Delia said, "Shit!—the English are so anti-semitic. Not in a crude way, on the whole. But in a snide, furtive way. As if being Jewish were a dirty joke."

"Religion's really a social thing, for *my* mama," said Johnny. "She goes to church on Sunday to meet her chums. Afterwards they have drinkies with each other, and little lunch parties."

"Both my parents are dead serious about it," said Delia. "And dead's the word. Shit! a lousy lifetime in exchange for the hope of a boring heaven." She poured what was left in the wine bottle into her glass. "Heaven!" she said, then "God!" then "Parents!"

Bettina said, "We've certainly lost the family piety of the Ancient Greeks. Think of Antigone guiding Oedipus all over the country after he'd blinded himself. And afterwards she was condemned to death for performing the funeral rites over the body of a brother she didn't even like."

"Fathers! Brothers! Yuck!" said Delia. Then she said, "And my dad believes he'll go to heaven. Shit!"

Bettina said, "Jews are very civilized about heaven. They tend to ignore it."

Johnny said, "Muslims get there by killing people. In

holy wars." He laughed. "I must say I prefer their heaven to the Christian one. Sex and sherbet and no-hangover wine in gorgeous gardens full of fountains. So much more amusing than choral singing on clouds with old aunts who've spent the time since they died learning to play the harp."

Bettina said, "Of course, mystics, whatever their religion, don't look at immortality in those crude terms."

"Mystics—shit!" said Delia. "All *they* do is induce hallucinations in themselves. When I was first in England, a woman I knew persuaded me to come to some weird conference. I didn't know what I was letting myself in for. There was this novelist who described how she'd achieved a mystical experience by shutting herself up in a bed-sitter and *starving*."

"Quite definitely not your line, Delia," said Johnny.

Delia finished her wine. She said, "We don't need gods. We need heroes."

Johnny said, "When I hear the word 'hero', I see a statue in a square. Wearing a sword and simply covered with pigeon-shit."

Delia said, "*I* think of freedom fighters."

"Freedom fighters!" said Johnny. "Those black men *coming*?"

"Yes. Coming to deliver the people."

Johnny laughed. "Deliver them from evil?"

"Yes. Exactly that," said Delia. Suddenly she stood up. "More than two hundred children killed by the South African police last year. More than two thousand detained, arrested, tortured."

"Young thugs with petrol bombs," said Johnny.

"*Children*. Shit!—I said *children*. And none of them had bombs." She turned and hurried across the terrace. Her towel-sarong fell to the ground; she ignored it. Reaching the mattress, she bent to scuffle in her raffia basket, and pulled out the pamphlet she had been reading that morning. "The reign of terror!" she exclaimed, coming, fast, back to the table. "The reign of terror!"

She came round the table to stand between Bettina and Johnny. She opened the pamphlet at a central section of photographs, held it open so that they could both see it. "Look!" she said. "Look!" Then, "Shit! Take off those damn dark glasses, Johnny."

He sighed. He shrugged. He took off the glasses. Delia leant forward, pointing at a photograph. "Look!" she said. "Look at that!"

Bettina drew in her breath. After a moment, Johnny said, "Reminds me of my public school," and Bettina drew in her breath again.

"Does it?" said Delia. "Oh, does it? When they beat you at your public school, did they do it with a sjambok? With a hide whip tipped with metal? Those dents you can see in this boy's flesh were made with that metal tip. Shit—that must have been quite some public school, Johnny." She turned a page. "And did they smash your front teeth, like this, with a rifle butt? Were your nails black and twisted like this from electric shock?"

Johnny said, "Of course, these pictures are obviously faked. It's just communist propaganda."

"Communist? Oh, really? This pamphlet was produced by a committee of American lawyers. It was published in New York. In your beloved USA!" She turned to the title page, and jabbed at the imprint with her finger, then turned to the photographs.

"Shit, Johnny, at your *public* school, did you have a burn like this on your wrist from a cigarette lighter? And did you have a wound like this on your leg where you were slashed with a broken bottle? Did those things happen to you, at your public school when you were eleven?"

Johnny said, "One isn't *at* one's public school at eleven. One's still at one's prep school."

Bettina closed her eyes, then opened them again. Delia turned another page. "Oh well, this boy's fifteen. Quite old enough for public school, but unfortunately he's a human vegetable, so I don't expect they'd want him. He was a normal boy, before the police took him in, and now he can hardly speak, and he doesn't understand what people say to him. When he walks, he shuffles, but, most of the time, he just sits, staring with those dead eyes. Dead," she repeated, and turned to a last picture. "Well at any rate, nobody *killed* you, Johnny. At your public school. I'm afraid I can't show you pictures of the children who died in detention, because their bodies were never released to their parents—I wonder why! And I haven't got a picture of the boy of thirteen who was grabbed by a policeman when he was on his way to school, and was beaten and trampled on, and died later, of internal injuries. And I haven't got pictures of the babies who died from tear-gas, when the police released a canister of it into a nursery school. But there is this picture of a four-year-old girl. Shit, Johnny—I don't think even you would suggest *she* was making petrol bombs. She was playing in the yard outside her house when a policeman fired a rubber bullet at her. Of course, rubber bullets aren't supposed to be lethal, but she died from brain damage. What does *that* mean to you, Johnny?"

Except for the thudding of the pamphlet in Delia's violently shaking hands, there was silence: of sea, of sky, of the terrace. Into that silence, Johnny—face and voice expressionless—spoke. "Nothing," he said, and then, "Nothing at all."

Now they were all quite still. Delia's hands had stopped shaking. They were all blank-faced in the silence. Suddenly, Bettina raised her hands and wrapped them round herself, clutching her upper arms, as if she were cold. Delia closed the pamphlet, and put it down on the table. A child stared on the cover. This child's eyes were not dead; they were alive with fear. Delia turned the pamphlet over. On the back, there was only print.

Johnny said, "It's marvellous, Delia, what indignation and concern you show for those children, when you obviously don't care a damn about your own child. I suppose it's because those ones are black."

Bettina brought her hands down again into her lap. Delia said, "I think I'll have a drop of brandy. Just to round off that wonderful meal." She paused, then said, "OK, Bettina?" as she moved towards the drinks trolley.

"Of course, Dee-dee. Help yourself to whatever you want."

Delia picked up the bottle of Rémy Martin. She half filled a small tumbler with it. Johnny glanced at Bettina, but she didn't look at him. She stared straight ahead, towards the rocks. Johnny's face twitched. He put on his dark glasses. Then he took a cigarette from his packet. He was lighting it as Delia came back to the table, and sat down. She took a sip of brandy. "Shit! This is great stuff," she said to Bettina. Then she took a gulp.

"I'm glad you like it." Bettina sighed. She said, "It's so hot." She raised her ivory crab, on its silver chain, took it off, and put it down on the table. "It feels heavy," she said.

Delia put out a finger and stroked it. "So smooth—the ivory," she said.

"It's an old Japanese ivory. A netsuke. Max bought it for me. He didn't like it much, but I knew it was for me, the moment I saw it. My birth sign, you know."

Johnny said, "I used to wonder why you didn't have a gold chain. But then I realized that gold would be quite wrong for you. You're a silver person, darling. Like the moon."

Bettina said to Delia, "I've been thinking of what you said about heroes. About our needing them, about their being freedom fighters, being deliverers. I think people have always seen them like that, in one way or another. But heroes can be very strange people. Think of Heracles."

"Hercules?" said Johnny. "He strangled snakes as a baby. Ugh! There was a picture of him doing it on a medicine bottle in my nursery."

Delia said, "It was called Woodward's Gripe Water, that medicine."

"Really?" said Johnny. "I only remember the snakes."

"Woodward's Gripe Water," Delia repeated. She drank some brandy. "It's still around. Woodward's Gripe Water. But they've changed the label. No more snakes."

Johnny said, "I'm delighted to hear it."

"I liked the old label," Delia said. "With the snakes."

"Heracles," said Bettina, "was the son of Zeus and of a queen called Alcmene, whose husband was away, fighting a war. Zeus was quite determined that the child was going to be a hero, and, when he went to bed with Alcmene, he turned three nights into one. Artists used to show her with three moons on her head. After the baby was born, Zeus tricked his wife, Hera, into suckling it, by putting it at her breast while she was asleep. When she woke, she was furious. It was she who sent those serpents to kill Heracles in his cradle. But, as you were saying, he strangled them. He was tremendously strong. As he grew up, he didn't recognize his own strength. By mistake, he killed one of his tutors, who was trying to teach him music, by hitting him on the head with a lyre."

Johnny said, "If only I'd thought of that when my mother made *me* have music lessons. Though, of course, a lyre's easier to handle than a piano."

"Heracles,'" said Bettina, "started his career as a hero early. He killed a wild beast that was terrorizing a whole region. He rescued a nation from paying an unjust tribute. One way and another, he became so famous that King Creon of Thebes gave him his daughter, Megara, as a wife, and made him governor of his kingdom.

"Heracles and Megara had eight children. Everything went well until the madness struck. Suddenly, one day, Heracles imagined that he was surrounded by strange enemies. He seized his bow and killed six of his children. When his mind cleared, and he understood what he'd done, he was shattered. He shut himself away in a dark place underground. But he emerged eventually—heroes have to—and went to seek purification. He consulted the Delphic Oracle. The Oracle directed him to go to serve a certain king. This king made him perform his twelve great labours. The Labours of Heracles. Don't worry—I won't describe them. It would take far too long. But he killed the Nemean lion. He captured the girdle of the Amazons. He stole the apples of the Hesperides." As she recited the names of these exploits, Bettina smiled, and closed her eyes. Opening them, she said, "Those were just three of the labours. After he'd accomplished all twelve, and was free again, he looked for a new wife. His previous marriage, to Megara, had broken down."

"Hardly surprising, in the circumstances," said Johnny. "After he'd killed all those kiddies of hers."

"He wanted a princess called Iole, but her father wouldn't allow it. Later, one of her brothers visited Heracles, and—in another of those fits of mad rage— Heracles murdered him. He hurled him from the roof of his house. To kill a guest—that was an almost unforgivable crime."

Johnny said, "Still is, darling, as far as I'm concerned."

"This time, when Heracles went to Delphi, the Oracle refused to pardon him. So—in a mad rage, of course—he desecrated the shrine. He stole its sacred tripod. He said that he would set up an oracle of his own. Apollo—the shrine at Delphi belonged to Apollo—came to kill him. Only the intervention of Zeus prevented it. Now the Delphic Oracle decreed that Heracles must be sold into slavery for three years. Omphale, Queen of Lydia, bought him. She made him dress as a woman and spin with her servants, while she covered herself with his lion-skin, and armed herself with his club. She often hit him with her sandals because of the clumsy way he held the distaff."

"He can't have looked his best in drag," said Johnny. "He was the 'Mr World' type, wasn't he?"

"Not on Greek vases. It was the Romans—typically! —who turned him into a muscle-bound heavyweight. And, apparently, swapping clothes became quite a habit with him and Omphale. Later, when their relationship developed into an affair, they used to do it when they travelled. Heracles was quite infatuated with her, but when his three years' slavery was at an end—off he set on his travels and adventures again. His hero's life. He killed a sea-monster and won a war. Eventually he settled down in Calydon where he married the local king's daughter."

"Awfully keen on the royals, wasn't he?" said Johnny.

"Well, after all, his father was the king of the gods. Anyway, everything went well until one of those mad rages ruined everything. He hit a young kinsman of his father-in-law, and killed him. He and his wife had to leave the kingdom. That was the journey that led to his death. When he was dying, in agony, from a poisoned garment he had been given, he ordered his funeral pyre to be built. He spread his lion-skin on top of it, and he lay down with his head resting on his olive-wood club." Bettina paused. Then she said, "A hero's life. A hero's death."

"So, was he burnt alive—poor chap?" asked Johnny.

"No, just as the pyre was lit, Zeus struck it with a thunderbolt and reduced it to ashes. Heracles was snatched up in a heavenly chariot to join the immortals on Olympus. But that part of the story doesn't interest me, so I was going to leave it out. What I'm haunted by is those strange fits of madness. So many powerful men have had them. Roman emperors. African dictators. Hitler. Stalin. *Paranoia*! The Greeks often blamed the gods for madness. They saw it as divine possession. So they made Hera responsible for the madness of Heracles, just as Dionysus was responsible for that of the maenads."

Delia said, "There's a strange disease that tribal Africans get. It's called *Ufufanyane*—the laughing sickness. It has all sorts of symptoms—shit!—fits, screaming, wild bursts of laughter, and running across country for mile after mile. I thought of it this morning when you were talking about the maenads. It's considered to be possession by a spirit. But, in *Ufufanyane*, the spirit has been sent by an enemy, using witchcraft."

Bettina said, "And is there a cure?"

"Only through the witchdoctor," said Delia. "It's an expensive illness. A cure can cost an ox."

Johnny laughed.

Delia said, "Conventional medicine hasn't been very successful in dealing with mental illness. Shutting people up in those dreadful hospitals like prisons. Playing electric roulette with their brains. Drugging them—though the drugs can help some people to get out of hospital and lead a kind of life outside."

"What sort of life?" said Bettina. Then, "Perhaps everything would have been different if Heracles and the maenads had been put on tranquillizers."

Delia laughed. "You can't confuse myth and reality, Bettina."

Bettina said, "Oh, can't I just!"

Johnny said, "Of course, a lot of loonies are just gaga." He raised the outer corners of his eyes with his forefingers, and dropped his jaw. "Uh, uh, uh, uh, uh," he grunted.

"We're not talking about congenital brain-damage," said Bettina, looking straight ahead. Although Johnny had been looking at her all the time she was telling the story of Heracles, she had not once looked at him.

"And then," he said, "there are the ones who think they're teapots or Napoleon. And then there are the mad murderers, of course." Hunching his shoulders and leaning back, with an expression of mock terror on his face, which he half shielded with his palms turned outwards, Johnny gave a low scream. "Otherwise"—here he reverted to his normal tone—"there are the idlers who think the State owes them a living. They sit around in doctors' waiting-rooms, hoping to talk about themselves or—better still—to be sent to hospital for a rest-cure."

"Some rest-cure. Shit!" said Delia. "But it's fascinating to hear *you* propagating the dignity of labour, Johnny."

"What I'm saying is perfectly true. There was a young man I knew. I put him up for a while. He was out of work, and I thought I'd give him a chance to get back on his feet. He was good-looking, quite bright in some ways, too —but you should have heard him when he got started on his symptoms. He was a walking medical dictionary. He said his hair was falling out, though there wasn't any sign of it—he had nice thick hair. Blond. He said his ears buzzed and his nasal passages were blocked. He said his teeth ground in the night. He said that he kept wanting to swallow, and that, every few minutes, his jaw would click out of position. He said the back of his neck ached. When I told him *he* was a pain in the neck, he was furious. He said his shoulders . . . but I won't go on. It would be too boring. The symptoms went all the way down to his feet—he had a sense of numbness in his toes. I took him to the South of France—I thought a change of scene might do him good."

Delia giggled. "Johnny the philanthropist!"

"But he became obsessed with a few mosquito-bites. He put a first-aid dressing on each bite—those little round dressings like corn-plasters. He looked as if he had plastic measles." Johnny frowned. "A lazy hypochondriac," he said angrily. "I had to kick him out. He was just no good."

Delia giggled again. "No good to you!" she said. She stood up. Her glass was empty. On the way to the drinks trolley, she said, "Johnny, you don't seem to have a clue about what madness means." Then, "Bettina—shit!—do you remember Elsie Stone? She taught English at varsity. Keen on Donne."

"Mmm. She had marvellous breasts, but she always wore baggy clothes—and used to stoop, as well—to hide them. Beautiful fair hair, but she dragged it back, and fastened it with an elastic band. No make-up."

"Shit!—that's Elsie! She was an idealist, a puritan, and she fell in love with a political. He was put inside for six years—communism. You described how she used to look most of the time—but I remember how she dressed up to visit him. With her hair built up into a tower, and sprayed stiff. Shit! And a jersey suit and high heels and lots of lipstick. I thought she looked terrible, as if she was wearing uniform. I used to wonder what *he* thought. She wasn't really involved in politics, herself. Of course she disapproved of apartheid, but she wasn't *active*. All the same, they took her inside at one stage. Solitary confinement. No charge. Long interrogations. The usual thing. People react to it in different ways, though." Standing by the trolley, Delia swayed a little. She said, "I've often wondered how I would have coped." Holding the bottle of Rémy Martin in her hand, she stared out to sea. "I'll never know," she said, and she poured brandy into her glass. "But it drove Elsie mad. Really mad. She thought they were putting ground-glass in her food, so she wouldn't eat anything. She thought there was poison in the water, so she tried not to drink. Then she started to believe they were puffing poison gas into her cell. Shit! —she even tried not to breathe! Well, they released her after only a couple of months, but they slapped a banning order on her so that she couldn't teach or lecture. In any case, she wouldn't have been able to—she was too ill. Even back outside she kept thinking she was being poisoned. Hell, she got terribly thin."

Delia came back to the table, with her full glass, and sat

down. She said, "People wanted Elsie to leave the country. She wouldn't, because of her visits to Tom. But then he died of a heart attack—he'd always had a bad heart —and Elsie came to England. At first she seemed a bit better. People organized a scholarship for her to do a Ph.D. But she couldn't concentrate. And she got more and more religious till one day she thought God told her to take off all her clothes in the street. So she did. Of course they put her in hospital. When she came out, she seemed better again, but then she tried to kill herself. This time they put her in another hospital."

Delia paused. Then she said, "After that, it was in and out again and again. I'd come to know her quite well. I must have visited her in at least six of those old London mental hospitals. *A rest-cure*! Shit, Johnny, if you'd ever been in one of those places, you wouldn't talk about rest-cures."

Delia gulped from her glass. "Each time Elsie came out, she'd wander North London like a pilgrim, looking for a place to stay till she got back on her feet and found a job. But she was so critical. If people had any luxuries in their houses, she'd tell them how wrong it was. And you could see she really enjoyed doing that. Her eyes would gleam sort of maliciously."

"Malice is part of madness," said Bettina.

"Yeah? Anyway people didn't like being lectured about how self-indulgent they were, especially politicals—they were the ones she used to go to. And they couldn't stand all the talk about God. Shit!—I didn't like it myself, but I felt so sorry for her. Sometimes I'd put her up. It was a bit uncomfortable, having only one room, but I'd sleep on the floor for a night or two and give her my bed. She used to cry in her sleep. I didn't know people could do that."

Delia drank again. Then she said, "There was one thing I really admired about Elsie. Shit!—as soon as she came out of hospital, she'd try to find some sort of job. As a filing-clerk or in a supermarket. And when she found a job she'd rent a room—you could still rent some sort of room cheaply in those days. But a job and a room couldn't save her. Down, down, down she'd go again. She'd take a lot of aspirins or make cuts in her wrists. Back to hospital. Then out again—another dreary job and ugly little room. Till, one Monday, I got a letter from her. It had been posted on Saturday. In the letter she said she was tired of being a nuisance to people, especially to me. She said she knew I found her a nuisance. I went round to her room. That time she'd managed to take enough pills. Her nose looked so big, sticking up over the sheet. Poor Elsie." Delia wiped her hand across her eyes then she said, "Shit, I felt guilty. Still do."

"You shouldn't," said Bettina. "You did all you could." She paused. Then she said, "I knew a composer who went mad. His wife supported him for two years while he wrote an opera. He was dreadful to her—always telling her what ugly legs she had and how stupid she was. And when he finished the opera, he couldn't find anyone to put it on." Bettina smiled. "He said you had to be homosexual or dead to have an opera performed. He treated his wife worse than ever. Then one day he saw a lion walking down the street. After that, he was always seeing it. He told his wife it was so much more attractive than she was. She got him to a doctor, and the doctor gave him pills. The pills stopped him seeing the lion, but then he gave up taking them because the lion was the only thing he wanted. The lion came back, but his wife left him. I haven't had any news of him for years. Last time I heard, he was living in a basement in North London. Somewhere called Tollington Park."

"With the lion, presumably." Johnny laughed.

"Shit!" said Delia. "I hate that Tollington Park. It gives me the creeps."

Johnny said, "There was a murder there—a famous murder. An awfully sordid man called Seddon killed his lodger so as to inherit her money. North London's very good for murder. There's Hilldrop Crescent where Crippen did his stuff. It was outside the Magdala pub in Hampstead that Ruth Ellis shot her lover. Mrs Pearcey slaughtered Phoebe Hogg in Ivor Street, Kentish Town—"

"Shit, man, how d'you know all this stuff?"

"Oh, it's a little hobby of mine. In London, as a whole, there are hundreds of houses where murders have been committed. They should put up blue plaques on them—but I suppose the owners might object."

"Yeah—they might indeed! But it's strange to think about what you've been saying. I walk in London a helluva lot at weekends—it's the only exercise I take. And some streets have a dreadful atmosphere. A sort of brooding gloom. I feel afraid when I walk down them. But murders can't have been done in all those streets. Have you ever heard of a murder in Highbury New Park, Johnny?"

"No," he said. "But of course there might have been an *undiscovered* one."

"Shit!—that's a street that frightens me. I don't know why. It's very quiet, with big houses. I've stopped walking down it. But I never had that weird feeling before I came to England—that fear! I never had it back home!"

"Oh God! She's harking back again," said Johnny.

Bettina was putting the coffee cups on the tray. She said,

"Suddenly I feel a bit tired. I'm going to have a little rest."

Johnny picked up the tray. He said, "I'll take that." He stooped for his bag, and went inside.

Bettina stood up slowly. "Are you going to have a rest, Dee-dee? Why don't you? Indoors. It's so stifling under this white sky."

"Nothing to read!" grumbled Delia. "I'm not in the mood for poetry yet."

Bettina laughed. "Take Piers. He'll put you to sleep, anyway."

"Yeah! Shit!" But she went over to the mattress, dropped the book about Piers into her basket, and put the basket over her arm. Back at the table, she picked up her nearly empty glass. "Think I'll refresh this. Take a little tot inside with me." She went over to the drinks trolley.

Bettina sighed. Then, "See you later," she said. Then, "Don't take any notice of Johnny. He doesn't mean half the things he says."

"I think you're wrong there. But—shit!—it doesn't bother me." Delia filled her glass with brandy as Bettina went indoors. When Bettina had gone, she said, "He's a filthy swine." Then, with drink and basket, she went into the house.

The sea looked dead under the heavy hazy sky. Johnny came out of the front door. He picked up Delia's pamphlet from the table. Holding it at arm's length, as if it were a dead rat, he carried it over to the waste-paper basket, and dropped it in.

He returned to the table. He picked up Bettina's crab pendant. Raising the chain in both hands, he put it over his head. The crab rested on the word *Ganglion*. Suddenly he slipped his arms out of his T-shirt, pulled it over his head, under the chain, and dropped it on the ground. Now the crab rested on his hairless chest, between the nipples, which were erect. Slowly, lightly, walking on the balls of his feet, he moved over to the rail, circling the crab between his fingers. Standing, looking out to sea, he released the crab, and raised both hands. He smoothed them over his hair, as if from a centre parting, then downwards and round, as if caressing a skein on his nape.

"Darling Bettina," he said.

"Darling Johnny," he answered, in a soft husky voice.

EVENING

It was almost dark. As Bettina came up the steps from the beach, her white towelling bathrobe seemed to shed light.

"Hullo there," said Johnny. His voice was quiet, to match the dusk. He leant on the rail, his bag on the ground beside him. He had changed into white jeans and a sea-green T-shirt; three black fishes swam across his chest.

"Hullo, Johnny," said Bettina. "What have you been doing?"

"Oh, I tidied the terrace." They both glanced round. His stretcher, Delia's mattress, and Bettina's table and chair had been put away.

"Very nice," she said.

"Afterwards, I lay down. I slept for half an hour, and then I read a thriller. The doctor was the murderer. Murder's easy for doctors. I'm sure they do it all the time."

Bettina said, "Delia thinks they're the new priests. You imagine them as killers. I see them as judges."

"Then I had a shower," Johnny said, "and changed, and came out here and watched you swimming. You slid into the water so gently that it hardly stirred. Then there was just your head, smooth as a seal's, and a glimpse or two of those little blue shoes. And when you came out you nestled into that bathrobe as if it were an ermine coat."

She came to stand beside him at the rail. "Hmm," she said. Then, "Not exactly ermine weather."

He said, "If I'd mentioned fur-coats to Delia, she would have given me a two-hour lecture on preserving wild life."

"Oh, stop it, Johnny. You scratch away at her as if she were an itch."

"She is, as far as I'm concerned," he said.

"It's not funny. And I asked you not to bait her."

They both leant on the rail, looking straight ahead. The three rocks were forming into a single dark mass. Johnny said, "Sorry, darling."

"I told you how truly horrible you were just after lunch. You were even worse later. Vile!"

"I'm really sorry." He glanced sideways at her profile. "You remind me of Garbo at the end of *Queen Christina*."

"What nonsense! There was a high wind blowing. And I haven't got that lovely straight blond hair, and my nose is thinner."

"I've always told you that you remind me of Garbo. Or perhaps I should say she reminds me of you. That's why I see her old films so often."

She said, "Well, I'm glad you chose *Queen Christina*, rather than *Camille*. That corpse-shot." With more emphasis, she said, "You know, you really shocked me this afternoon."

He glanced sideways again. "She makes me say things I don't mean."

"That's what I told her. I hope it's true."

"Really it is, darling."

"I suppose I must take your word for it." Simultaneously, they turned towards each other. His smile was eager; hers was hesitant, qualified.

"Hey, Bettina."

They both looked round as Delia came out of the house. She was still wearing her red bathing-dress. In her hand was her empty brandy glass.

"*Hi*, Delia." Johnny's enthusiasm sounded inordinate.

Delia looked startled. "How are you feeling?" he said. "Have you been asleep?" His vehement interest made Bettina press her lips together as if quelling a smile.

Delia said, "I feel all right. A bit dazed. I'm not used to sleeping in the afternoon." She turned to Bettina. "You've been swimming?"

"Yes."

Delia said, "These solitary dips! It's sad we never swim together."

Bettina said, "Swimming together presents problems. Johnny likes to swim in the midday sun—"

"*Mad dogs and Englishmen.* . . ." sang Johnny.

"And you, Dee-dee, go in straight after lunch because your father wouldn't let you."

Delia said, "Do you think that's the reason? Shit!" She set off for the drinks trolley. "Perhaps you're right."

"And I," said Bettina, "prefer dawn or dusk."

"The pearly girl," said Johnny.

"Pearly girl?" said Delia.

Johnny said to Bettina, "I remember you once singing, 'Pearly one morning'—"

"Instead of 'Early'?" Delia broke in.

"Correct!" He went on, "And I asked you why, and you said that everything—the sky, the sea, even the land—was pearly at sunrise and at sunset."

"*Pearly one morning, just as the sun was rising,*" Bettina sang in a small soprano. She broke off, said, "Fancy your remembering that, Johnny."

"I remember most things you say."

"Johnny Boswell's Life of Bettina Johnson," said Delia.

Bettina said, "It's not pearly this evening. There's just a deepening grey."

"Dark, soon," said Delia. She had poured her brandy,

and came to stand, next to Bettina, at the rail. "Perhaps," she said, "tonight, I'll plunge at midnight. I used to love doing that. I was telling Johnny before lunch how I used to swim at night in a rock pool, back home." Taking her first gulp of brandy, she made a spontaneous grimace, gave an involuntary shiver of shock. Then she said, "Do you think the sea will be warm enough, Bettina?"

"I'm sure it will. It's very warm and sticky now. In a moment, I shall go to have my bath."

"You're as bad as Johnny." Delia took another gulp of brandy; this time she showed no reaction.

"What do you mean?" said Johnny. "As bad as me?"

Bettina said, "Oh, Delia has this theory that having baths and showers is neurotic."

"Unnecessary baths and showers," said Delia. "Typical of white South Africans. They're always washing their guilt away. Like Lady Macbeth. Like Pontius Pilate. But it's more than that. I think they want to wash the pigment out of their skins."

Johnny said, "I've never heard such rubbish in my life. Doesn't it occur to you Delia that *some* people simply like to be clean?"

Bettina said, "Of course, there's an element of spiritual purification in the background. Baths have always been part of rituals. Look at baptism. And the *mikvah*. That's the Jewish ritual bath. I had to have one when I converted. Orthodox women go to the *mikvah* every month—a week after they menstruate. Until then, they can't have any sexual contact with their husbands. They're unclean."

Delia said, "What a degrading idea. Shit!"

"Degrading? I suppose so. Primitive, certainly." Bettina smiled. "Converts are seen as Jewish souls trapped in Gentile bodies. The first *mikvah* sets them free. A very close resemblance to baptism, there." She paused, smiled again. "You know, I loved my *mikvah*. You have to make all sorts of preparations for it. The waters of the *mikvah* have to touch every part of your body. First, you have an ordinary bath and a shower. There mustn't be a particle of food stuck between your teeth—and if you wear false ones, you have to take them out. There mustn't be a scrap of grime under your nails, and of course you mayn't wear nail varnish. Every crevice and orifice must be spotless. You must blow your nose. You must comb your washed hair. You work your way through a whole programme. A list. The last words on it are: 'Now you are ready for the great *mikvah* of *Tevilah*'—*Tevilah* means immersion." She repeated, "The great *mikvah* of *Tevilah*!" She smiled. "The water of the *mikvah* seemed so soft—there has to be a lot of rainwater in it. You stand in the bath with your feet and arms apart, and then you go down, down, under the water. You do that three times. Some people go down horizontally. Others curl up, as if they were in the womb. That was what I did. Strange!" She paused. She said, "Afterwards, I felt so vulnerable. Like a snail without its shell. But so pure and gentle. I felt at peace."

Delia said, "Did you ever have another *mikvah*?"

Bettina shook her head. "No, that was the only one. Max wasn't Orthodox. He asked me to convert for tribal rather than religious reasons. He wanted to reconcile his relations to the marriage. I had to learn some Hebrew, too. I've forgotten every word of that. But I remember the *mikvah*." She paused, then laughed. "It would have been terrible to be Orthodox. All those separate sets of china and absurd cookery regulations. Worst of all, I would have had to shear my head and wear a *sheitl*—that's a wig.' She shuddered.

"Absolutely out of the question," said Johnny.

"Shit!—it's all so ludicrous," said Delia.

Bettina said, "Of course, a bath doesn't have to be a ritual. The Romans bathed a lot, just for fun."

"And Americans do," said Delia. "Perhaps it's an imperialist characteristic. Those Victorian Englishmen never stopped having cold baths."

"What rubbish," muttered Johnny.

Bettina said, "I had a wonderful Turkish bath in Istanbul. Pure pleasure. The woman in charge was obviously a retired prostitute. She wore a skirt, but nothing above it except a lot of gold chains. A lifetime's savings, I suppose. And her tired old breasts hung down under the chains. After I'd steamed, she massaged me with crushed olives. It's amazing how much dirt rolls out of one's skin."

"Even *your* skin?" said Johnny.

"Even mine, darling," said Bettina.

"Around the world in eighty baths," said Delia. Then, "Charlotte Corday killed Marat in his bath."

"And there were the 'Brides in the Bath' murders," said Johnny. "Glup, glup, glup. Smith had a good idea, but he shouldn't have repeated it. That was his undoing. He should have found other methods." Johnny laughed. "After one of the murders, his landlady heard him playing 'Nearer, my God, to Thee' on the harmonium."

Bettina said, "Agamemnon was having a bath when Clytemnestra killed him. That was a ritual bath—he was purifying himself after the Trojan war. Aeschylus says the bath was made of silver, and that Clytemnestra netted him in a robe to stop him struggling while she and her lover stabbed him."

"Awfully unsporting," said Johnny.

Delia said, "I've always felt a lot of sympathy for Clytemnestra. After all, Agamemnon had murdered their daughter just to get a fair wind to sail to Troy."

"Sacrificed her," said Bettina.

"Same thing. Shit! And then he brought that useless, boring Cassandra home as his mistress."

"Useless? Boring?" said Bettina.

"Yeah. What's the use of prophesying if nobody believes you? It's just a bore."

Bettina said, "Clytemnestra evidently agreed with you. When she'd finished off Agamemnon, she killed Cassandra."

Delia said, "And then there was that terrible second daughter, Electra. Shit! She didn't care a stuff about her father murdering her sister. All she was interested in was egging on little brother Orestes to murder their mother."

"Electra had loved her father," said Bettina. Then, "Greek audiences always cheer when Electra and Orestes are reunited, after years of separation. They're on her side."

"Well," said Delia, "I'm not."

"You know," said Johnny, "I think I agree with Delia—"

"Shit! I don't believe it!"

"Just this once," he said. "Murdering one's mama really seems to me rather beyond the pale, let alone being pushed into it by one's elder sister. Elder sisters are awfully tiresome—I should know. One must never let them push one around. And after Orestes killed his mother, I think it was quite right for those Furies we were talking about this morning to get on his trail. *I* think they should have grabbed him. Not let him go."

"Then they wouldn't have become the Kindly Ones," said Bettina.

"They never did. As I said this morning—a likely story! Those Furies are still around today." He laughed. "And there isn't a Kindly One among them."

Bettina said, "Perhaps you're right." Then she said to Delia, "I admit that Electra nags and whines a bit. And I have some sympathy for Clytemnestra. Most people hate her. But people always hate and fear great queens, powerful women. Like the Queen of the Night in *The Magic Flute*."

Delia said, "I've never seen it. I always thought it was an opera for children."

"Far from it. So many people think of Mozart as light and charming. Actually he can be quite terrifying."

"Yeah," Delia said thoughtfully. "He can. Shit!"

"The Queen of the Night is gorgeous. She glitters. And she pits herself against freemasonry, which the opera glorifies. Freemasonry is a male cult, and though the music is so beautiful, the opera is full of insults to women and contempt for them. The Queen of the Night personifies women as bold and daring and powerful. The chief mason calls her 'a woman who thinks too highly of herself, and who hopes to bring down our temple.' He steals her daughter." Bettina paused. "One character calls her 'The star-radiant queen.' Of course, she is destroyed in the end."

"Of course," said Delia.

"But now I'm definitely going to have my bath. Come on, Dee-dee, why don't you have one, too? It'll brighten you up after your sleep." Bettina turned from the sea, and started to cross the terrace. She said, " 'Changes of raiment and the warm bath are dear to us ever.' That's what Homer says."

"Really, darling," said Johnny. "Talk about being soaked in the classics!"

"It's true. I'm soaked. I'm immersed. They're my *mikvah* of *Tevilah*." She laughed. "But only in translation, alas. How I wish I knew Ancient Greek instead of just a little modern demotic."

"Why don't you learn?" said Delia.

"Too late."

"Oh, shit! What crap!"

"Too late." Bettina was standing by the table. Now she picked up her necklace, which was lying curled in a clean ashtray, and swung the pendant like a pendulum. "Come on, Dee-dee. Warm bath and change of raiment." She laughed.

At the beguiling sound of this laugh of Bettina's—soft and breathy—Delia smiled. "Oh, why not?" she said. "Dressing for dinnah, what? Frafly posh."

"I don't know about *dinner*," said Bettina. "I thought we'd have something light after that fairly large, late lunch."

"Oh, of *course*. That's *fine*." Delia spoke with much emphasis.

"Though *you*, darling," Johnny said to Bettina, "ate hardly anything."

"Oh, I had enough. I'm not at all hungry now. Later, perhaps."

"Later, I shall make some awfully appealing little sandwiches to tempt you."

"Perfect! Johnny makes the most exquisite sandwiches, Dee-dee."

"I'm *sure* he does. Too, too exquisite for words." As Bettina went indoors, switching on the light in the hall, Delia drank what was left in her glass. She hesitated, glancing towards the drinks trolley, but then put her glass down on the table, and followed Bettina into the house.

Alone on the terrace, Johnny leant back against the rail. He folded his arms, and scratched his biceps. The muscle at the corner of his mouth twitched.

Light came on in Delia's window, under the awning. The pattern of the window's wrought-iron guard stood out dark against a thin blond curtain, across which, now, Delia's shadow passed. Johnny made a two-fingered gesture at this shadow, and it moved out of sight.

Now he strode to the front door, and flicked a switch just inside, turning on the lamp that hung above the terrace table. The lamp's fall of light conformed exactly to the table's circumference. Everything beyond was dim, arboreal: under the vine and in the green glow of the lamp's opaque glass shade.

On the table, Delia's smudgy glass was limelit, and Johnny grimaced at it. He went over to the drinks trolley. There, he held the Rémy Martin bottle up to the light. It was nearly empty. He smiled, and put it down. He took the lid off the ice-bucket, and emptied the water from it over the side rail of the terrace where vine trailers hung down. He replaced the lid, and put the bucket in the crook of his left arm. He picked up the Rémy Martin bottle and put it in the waste-paper basket. Carrying the basket, he went to the table, and paused there, resting the basket on it. Light shone on the brandy bottle and caught the eyes of the child on the cover of Delia's pamphlet, next to the bottle. Now, with the same disdain he had shown earlier, when handling the pamphlet, Johnny picked up Delia's glass and deposited it in the basket. Then—ice-bucket held in the curve of his left arm, rim of the waste-paper basket grasped in his right hand—he marched into the house.

For a few minutes, the terrace was entirely quiet. Then a moth fluttered round the lamp bulb. From far off, came a low rolling sound which died away as the moth's body drifted on to the table. Johnny came out of the house with the ice-bucket, the waste-paper basket and a fresh bottle of brandy. He put the ice-bucket on the trolley and the basket on the floor. He removed the bottle's foil seal and dropped it into the basket. Then he put the new bottle where the old one had stood.

Now, as, scratching his biceps, he looked round the terrace, Johnny's glance was caught by the dead moth. With a tissue, he went over to the table and picked up its body, which he took back and dropped into the waste-paper basket. Then he stooped for two objects on the lower shelf of the trolley: a spiked square of tin in a pottery bowl and a bright cardboard packet—blue, yellow, red and green—with a leopard pictured on it in an aggressive pose. From this packet he extracted a matt green disc. He fingered this deftly, and it separated into two coiled snakes, each with a rounded head and a slit eye. He replaced one snake in the packet, which he put back on the lower shelf. Then he impaled the other, through its eye-slit, on the tin spike. He took his lighter from his pocket, snapped it on, and held the flame to the snake's tail. The tail blazed for a moment. Then the flame went out, but now the tail-tip glowed orange, and a thin line of smoke rose into the air. Johnny put away his lighter. Carrying the bowl in both hands, he went over to the table, squatted down, and put the bowl underneath.

Standing up, he looked round the terrace again. He folded his arms, and scratched his biceps. The muscle at the corner of his mouth twitched. He took cigarettes from his pocket, and lit one. Smoking, he walked to and fro between the table and the rail of the terrace several times. Then he picked up his bag from beside the rail, and went quickly indoors.

The lampshade glowed green; the table was a yellow circle of light; underneath, the snake's tail of the insect-coil burned orange. Now the dimmer, curtained rectangle of Delia's window went dark, and a moment or two later she came out onto the terrace.

She wore a red cotton dress: bell-shaped, and with bell sleeves. The round neck was cut low, but the cleft between her breasts was covered by the black, green and yellow square, with a white fringe, at the end of an African bead necklace. She had washed her hair. It hung, damp, but combed, to her shoulders. She was wearing bright red lipstick.

She glanced round, then set off for the drinks trolley; her backless wedge-heeled sandals clacked on the paving. At the trolley, she took one of the small tumblers, and then picked up the brandy bottle. Surprised by its weight, she held it up to the light and saw that it was full. She peered about for the old bottle, then frowned, shrugged, and pulled out the cork of the new one. She glanced towards the front door, then raised the bottle to her mouth, tilted back her head, and swigged. Lowering the bottle, she closed her eyes. Opening them again, she shook her head as if to clear it. Then she poured a large tot of brandy into the tumbler. She paused, put down the bottle, then took the lid off the ice-bucket. With her fingers, she dropped two ice-cubes into her drink. She went to the table, where she sat down in the same chair she had sat in earlier. She took a sip from her glass, then put it down on the table, on which she now rested her elbows. Propping her jaw on her hands, she stared down into the brandy.

"Hullo, Dee-dee." Delia looked up as Bettina came out of the house. She wore a black kaftan. She seemed all black and white, except for her eyes, her pink mouth, her silvered nails, and her ivory pendant on its silver chain.

Delia said, "The Queen of the Night! Is that how she looked?"

"Rather more jewellery," said Bettina, sitting down with her back to the front door. "Diamonds, and so on. 'Star-radiant,' you know. You look nice. I like that dress. The colour's good. Your necklace doesn't go with it."

"Shit! I love this necklace. It's in the people's colours. Green for the grass, yellow for the sun, black for the people."

"Yes, I see. Anyway, I like the dress. The sleeves are pretty. No woman over thirty-five should wear sleeveless dresses.

"Shit!—one never gets the chance in England."

"Or bikinis."

Delia sighed. "I've always had enough sense to avoid those. Sometimes I think I should cut my hair? Don't you think I'm too old for long hair?"

"Certainly not. Not for another five years, at least, and then you must cut it only a little. So that it doesn't touch your shoulders. That draws too much attention to one's neck. More than slightly shorter hair does. But middle-aged women with really short hair look like ancient children." She smiled. "Like Johnny's bare ruined choirboys. Do you tint it?"

"No. So far I've only one or two grey hairs. But when it goes grey, I don't know if I can be bothered, except that people think of grey-haired women as old. I know a woman of fifty whose hair's almost white. She's a very lively, energetic person, but I heard some man describe her as 'a nice old lady.' I'm sure it was because of her hair. Shit! I wouldn't like that."

Bettina said, "Well, if you do decide to tint it, gradually make it brown. Don't keep it black. Black's too hard for an older face. So are yellow and red. They seem to make the wrinkles show up more. Brown, ash-blond, a soft Veronese—not Titian—are the only possibilities."

Delia laughed. "You sound like a posh fashion magazine. Or a mother giving her daughter the benefits of a lifetime's experience. Not that my mother did that. Shit! —all she wanted was to stop me wearing make-up or sexy clothes."

Bettina said, "For me, it's a question of aesthetics."

Delia waved a vague hand in the air. "Smart clothes, make-up, hair-styles—what's the point really? They're unnecessary." Then she gave a loud surprised laugh. "Shit! Why, I sound like my mother. God forbid! But I've never been like you—really interested in fashion."

"Not *fashion*. Fashion's so often silly or vulgar . . . though sometimes a designer transcends—seems to transcend—that. But I suppose you could say I've always been interested in looking elegant."

"You always do look elegant. You do now. Though, these days—except when you came to meet me at the airport in those white trousers with that blue tunic on top—you never seem to wear anything but this one design of kaftan. How many of them have you got?"

Bettina laughed. "Oh, about twenty, I think."

"Shit! But you used to wear different kinds of clothes at different times of day. You were always changing your clothes."

"I still change my kaftans. But I've been trying to simplify things."

"Yeah? With twenty kaftans?"

Bettina laughed. "Yes, it's a lot. But it's still a simplification."

Delia said, "Like you've been simplifying your books and records?"

"In a way."

"And I suppose it's the same with pictures, is it?"

"Mmm."

"That's more than *simplifying*, though. No paintings at all. Just that little one in my bathroom, of all places!"

Bettina said, "Oh, well, the colours are right for a bathroom: shit-brown and piss-yellow."

There was a moment's pause. Delia said, "It's weird, but I feel quite shocked when you use words that I say all the time."

"That's because I use them so rarely. Only when they're entirely appropriate."

Delia took a gulp from her glass. Now it was almost empty. "But seriously," she said, leaning forward, "*seriously*, why don't you put up any of your other paintings?"

"I've disposed of them. I don't paint any more." Johnny, unheard, unseen, appeared behind her in the doorway as she said, "Having those old pictures of mine on the walls would be like having discarded lovers hanging about the house."

"Discarded lovers? What a fascinating conversation," said Johnny as he reached the table.

Bettina looked up at him. "Hullo, Johnny." She sounded relieved. Then she said, "Not as fascinating as you imagine."

"Very fascinating, *I* thought." Delia finished her brandy.

"Drinkies-time," said Johnny. "What do people want?"

Bettina said, "What's that you've been drinking, Delia? Brandy?"

Delia nodded.

"Very bad for you, darling," said Bettina. "Why don't you share a bottle of white wine with me? I know Johnny always has vodka and tonic at this time of day."

Delia frowned. Then, after a moment, she said, "Well, yeah."

"I'll fetch it," Johnny said, and went indoors.

Now Delia said, "You worked so *hard* at it." Again she leant forward, with an earnest look.

"At what?"

"Shit! Your painting, of course."

Bettina gave a small cross grunt. "Oh, *that*." Then she said, "Anyway, my work would probably never have been good enough. And it's too late to find out now."

"What crap!"

"Too late!" Bettina's oracular tone was followed by a silence in which Delia fidgeted with her empty tumbler.

Johnny came out of the house carrying a tray on which were two wine glasses, and an opened bottle of white wine. Delia, watching him fill the glasses, said to Bettina, "Forty's no age nowadays. For a lot of women that's when a whole new life begins."

"*Quel cliché!*" said Johnny.

Delia said, "Clichés are often true."

"And that's *another* cliché. I'd say that, for most women, forty's when life ends." He put one glass in front of Bettina, the other in front of Delia, who picked it up at once. He went on, "The *kiddies* are leaving home. *Hubby*'s busy with his career and his new secretary. *Wifey*'s losing her looks and hasn't a clue what to do with herself."

"Shit! What a crude, bourgeois, sexist picture!" said Delia. She drank some wine. At the taste of it, her face took on a dissatisfied expression.

Bettina said, "I must say, you make things sound pretty hopeless for us, Johnny."

He looked horrified. "Darling, surely you know I wasn't talking about *you*. It never entered my mind. Of course I think of you as ageless."

Bettina said, "That word always makes me think of *embalmment*."

"But I didn't mean—" His shoulders tensed. The muscle at the corner of his mouth twitched.

"Don't get so agitated." She smiled. "Fool!" she said, and he relaxed and smiled back at her.

Delia, though still looking dissatisfied, was drinking her wine. "Lots of women take the opportunity to begin new lives at forty," she said.

"OK, OK—you've said that already. And spare us the speech on Women's Lib." Johnny went over to the drinks trolley. "Oh!" he exclaimed. "Someone's left the lid off the ice-bucket."

"Guess who?" said Delia.

"I don't have to *guess*."

Delia said, "It can't have melted much. Anyway, who cares? Granny Fairfield cares, that's who. Fuss, fuss, fuss, he goes."

Johnny, pouring vodka, said, "Perhaps you'll be a granny yourself, one of these days. To a whole troop of dear little right-wing churchgoers."

Bettina said, "Stop it."

Johnny busied himself with his drink. Delia said to Bettina, "Of *course* it isn't too late for you to start painting again."

Bettina said, "Oh, Delia, you don't know what you're talking about."

Johnny came back to the table with his long, pretty drink. He said, "I've always loved your paintings, Bettina. So decorative! I certainly think you should do some more." He sat down next to her, opposite Delia.

"Decorative," murmured Bettina.

"Decorative!" shouted Delia. "Shit! Bettina's paintings were much more than that."

"Were they?" Again Bettina murmured; perhaps she was talking only to herself.

Johnny said to Delia, "I don't see what's wrong with things being decorative. Surely that's what art's for? To be attractive?"

"Oh, God," said Delia. "Art's about truth, not attractiveness. Art's serious."

"Oh, God," said Johnny. "Truth, indeed! What's truth? Anyway, who wants a crucifixion over the sofa? I'd much rather have a Dufy."

"Oh, well—shit—a *crucifixion*," said Delia. "I agree. Though I don't much like Dufy. He paints the same pictures over and over again."

"I've got three of Bettina's lovely paintings," said Johnny.

"I haven't got any." Delia sounded downcast.

"I didn't know you wanted one," said Bettina. "You never asked."

"What other pictures have you got?" Delia asked Johnny. "Besides Bettina's."

"Oh, well, there's the Dufy. And then I have another friend, apart from Bettina, who's a painter. He goes to country houses, and does pictures of them. Awfully charming. Of course, the owners of the houses buy the paintings. But I have several of his sketches and water-colours."

"Shit! Is that how he earns his living?"

Bettina laughed. "You make him sound like a pimp or a pusher, Dee-dee. I can think of far worse occupations than painting country houses."

Johnny said, "He makes a very *good* living. And of course it's a very pleasant way of life. Staying with charming people in beautiful surroundings."

Delia groaned. "Yuck," she said. Then, "Nothing to do with what *I* mean by an artist."

Johnny said, "What *do* you mean by an artist, Delia?"

Delia said, "Someone who suffers."

Bettina blinked. Johnny said, "Goodness!"

Delia said, "I think of Jake Molefe. A wonderful artist. Shit! I've got one of his pictures. A woman standing in a forest."

"With a piece of pottery on her head?" said Johnny.

"No pottery, Johnny. She's at one with the forest. The leaves caress her. The branches embrace her."

"Coo-er!" said Johnny.

"I remember the painting," said Bettina. "In your room. Over the mantelpiece. I liked it. So many different greens and browns. And a touch of red somewhere, isn't there?"

"That's right. A red bird."

"Robin Redbreast!" said Johnny.

Delia said, "Oh, shit, man!" Then, to Bettina, "Jake had to struggle so, to become an artist. He was so poor. And he found it so difficult to get any recognition. The few of us who bought his pictures couldn't afford to pay proper prices for them. And posh people who wanted *just a touch of Africa, doncher know* as part of their decor always seemed to buy pictures of Africans by white artists. Professors of Art, usually—I suppose their academic qualifications were reassuring. Shit! One night Jake went back to the location alone. It was pitch dark—no street-lighting, of course. A gangster stabbed him for his money. I heard it was about five rand. He was only twenty-four. Ah, shit! They say the dogs drank his blood in the gutter." For a moment, Delia pressed her hands over her face.

"I suppose the gangster was black," said Johnny.

"Yeah. Sure to have been. A *tsotsi*. Does that prove something, Johnny? I can't think what."

Bettina said, "I've known a lot of artists. But the only ones I can think of at this moment are all failures. There was Micky van Rooyen. There was that composer who saw a lion."

"In Tollington Park," murmured Delia.

"In Murderland," said Johnny.

"The third is quite a different case. In one sense, he's a success. Snell."

"Snell?" said Johnny.

"Yes, L. K. Snell. The novelist."

Delia said, "Shit! I read one of his books. I couldn't stand it."

Bettina said, "I would have expected that. In his four big novels, his targets are your beliefs. Liberation of blacks, of women, of colonial territories. He shows the liberators themselves as utterly corrupt and their ideals as absurdly sentimental. The books are wonderfully written. They've been greatly praised. Yet they make me think of what you said this morning, Johnny, about a snake sliming its prey. Snell slimed his characters so that he could swallow them. And then he disgorged them. He spat them out. But now he writes topical travel books about Third World countries—about how their ideals are absurdly sentimental and they are utterly corrupt. He can't write novels any more. Creatively, Snell has slimed himself out."

Johnny had grimaced at Bettina's mention of the snake, but now he said, "Perhaps I'll try one of those novels. They sound awfully interesting."

Delia said, "I thought you didn't read novels. Apart from *crime*, of course."

Johnny said, "I often read *Brideshead Revisited*."

"*Brideshead Revisited*?" said Bettina.

"*Brideshead Revisited*!" said Delia.

"Yes. I read it once a year. Now *that*'s what *I* call a well-written book."

Bettina said, "I prefer Waugh's early work."

Delia said, "You'll be turning to Rome soon, Johnny. I think Lord Marchmain's death is even funnier than Little Nell's."

Bettina laughed.

Johnny said, "I think it's a brilliant book. Brilliant, and perfectly beautiful."

"Shit!" said Delia. "All that stuff about sin, and setting up a rival good to God's."

Bettina said, "I sometimes think that's what every artist does. Go into competition with God. That's why your Muslim friends, Dee-dee, are so nervous of art, as opposed to artefacts. They suspect that artists are trying to outdo Allah." She paused. Then she said, "Prometheus was the first artist."

Delia said, "He was a hero. He stole fire for the human race."

Johnny said, "Most unwise. A vulture kept pecking at his liver. Awfully disagreeable."

"He was an artist," said Bettina. "According to one myth he created humankind. He moulded a man and a woman out of clay. Then he persuaded Athene to breathe life into them, and Zeus was enraged. But the other myth, the more common one, doesn't go so far as that. It doesn't make Prometheus our creator. It just tells how he used his skill and cunning to outwit Zeus on our behalf. Prometheus was always on our side. For instance he was determined that people should have the better part of every sacrifice they offered to the gods. So he made two very ingenious bundles out of the carcass of an ox. One bundle was the hide and the bones, wrapped in fat. The other was all the best meat, packed inside the stomach. Prometheus asked Zeus to choose which he wanted, and Zeus chose the one wrapped in succulent fat. You can imagine how angry he was when he found nothing but skin and bones inside. It was in revenge that Zeus concealed the secret of fire. However, Prometheus stole the fire for us from heaven, and, after that, went on to teach us all the arts and skills that distinguish us from other animals. Meanwhile, of course, Zeus became more and more angry."

"Shit! Typical of a father god," said Delia. "Just like it was in the Garden of Eden when Adam and Eve were punished for wanting knowledge. I suppose you could say that, in a way, Satan was a kind of Prometheus."

"Well, both of them were working against the top god, but Satan wasn't working for *people* like Prometheus. Satan didn't take risks for us, as Prometheus did when he roused the fury of Zeus, who became determined to be revenged on him. And now the myth we're talking about has a strange echo of that other one I mentioned—the one where Prometheus created people out of clay. But here it was Zeus who ordered a woman to be made of clay, and then told Athene—Athene again!—to breathe life into it. When she'd done so, Zeus called on all the gods to give the woman gifts of beauty and charm, and to make her irresistibly attractive. Then he sent her to earth. She was called Pandora."

"The one with the box full of horrors," said Johnny.

"It was a vase, actually."

"Anyway, there was Hope at the bottom," said Delia.

"Yes," says Bettina, "there was Hope at the bottom. Anyway, Prometheus resisted the irresistible Pandora, but his brother yielded to her, and all those miseries—plus Hope, of course, Delia—were let loose on us. So, in a sense, Zeus won that round against our champion, Prometheus. But then they had another dispute, at the end of which Zeus had Prometheus chained to that rock. Every day the vulture tore his liver. Every night his liver healed in order to be torn again next day."

"Shit! What happened then?"

"No one's quite sure. Shelley wrote a play in which Prometheus defeated Zeus—just your style, Dee-dee. But that was rather late in the day. In the play by Aeschylus, Prometheus was left chained to the rock. But that play was only the first part of a trilogy, and the other two parts have disappeared. The general consensus is that Prometheus was freed in the end—by our old friend, Heracles—and that he and Zeus were reconciled. The Greeks believed in reconciliation."

"Not like our God and Satan," said Delia. "At war for ever! Shit!"

Johnny sighed. He was scratching his biceps. "You know," he said, "I think I'm going to make those sandwiches now. Like Heracles, I'm ready for a little labour. I can cover them with cling-film if we don't want to eat just yet."

"I can just imagine Heracles with a roll of *cling-film*," said Delia. Then, as Johnny went into the house, taking his unfinished vodka and tonic with him, she picked up the wine bottle and, her eyebrows raised, held it in the air over Bettina's still half-full glass. Bettina shook her head, and Delia put the bottle down. "Somehow," she said, "*I* don't feel like any more wine, either." Not looking at Bettina, she said, "I think I'll have another tot of brandy." Standing up, she said, "He's a strange one—old snaky. Shit! I don't think I'll ever understand him.

"Johnny?"

"Yeah. Now, this morning, when you were resting, he was so fucking sweet to me. You know, I even thought perhaps we might become friends."

"*Really?*"

"Yeah." She was pouring brandy into her tumbler when the low rolling that had sounded earlier recurred, a little louder. "Like a tumbril," she said, looking up.

Bettina said, "Have you ever heard a tumbril?"

Delia laughed. "No, but that's what I imagine it would sound like. What was it?"

"Thunder."

"Oh! Are we going to get a storm? From your friend Zeus?"

"Perhaps. Go on about Johnny."

"Oh, yeah." Carelessly, Delia had filled her tumbler with brandy to the very brim, and now she bent her head down to the trolley, and drank a little, so that she could pick up the glass without spilling its contents. Coming back to the table with it, she said, "Shit! He explained that whole thing that had always stuck in my gullet. That time when I asked to borrow money, and he refused."

"You asked Johnny for money? You never told me that—nor did he. Why didn't you ask *me*?"

"You were away somewhere. Travelling. In the Caribbean, I think it was. I was desperate."

"I can't imagine why those people don't pay you a decent salary."

"Oh, they've offered me more, but I can't take it. When I think of what the money's being raised for, how can I live in luxury?"

"I didn't say anything about *luxury*. I just meant without having to worry about money. And you work so hard. After all"—now Bettina smiled—"'To each according to his work.'"

"I've never really liked that. I've always preferred the original: 'To each according to his need.' Anyway, I manage OK most of the time. But—shit!—this was an emergency. So I rang up Johnny."

"Rang him up? That's always a mistake. He hates the telephone. He says it's an intrusion. Like a person walking into one's house without being invited."

"Why does he have a phone, then?"

"Oh, just for making practical arrangements."

"Shit! It's in character," said Delia. "Two kinds of people hate the telephone. People who are very shy. Stammerers, and so on. You can't blame *them*. And people who want to prove how *cool* they are—that's Johnny. Chatting on the phone is too friendly to be cool. Anyway, my call to him *was* practical. I just wanted to borrow this money, though of course I asked him how he was, and so on, first."

"How much did you want?"

"A hundred pounds. I told him I really needed it."

"If you hadn't needed it, he'd probably have lent it to you."

Delia looked puzzled. "Shit! That sounds weird. Anyway, as he told me this morning, he just couldn't manage it at the time."

"Couldn't manage it? There's never been a moment in Johnny's life when he couldn't have lent someone a hundred pounds."

"Really? Are you sure? He said he'd been ill, and he was out of work. And of course I know his money from back home has dried up."

"Dried up? What nonsense! Of course, the value of the rand is low, and one has to pay a huge tax to take out more than a certain amount. But that old vampire mother of his is really very rich indeed. *Old* money." Bettina laughed. "Not like Max's. Lots and lots of it, too. She sends him money all the time. How else do you think he could afford that flat in Chelsea?"

"I know it's a posh address, but—shit!—I've never been there. What's it like?"

"Oh, it's a mixture. Fitted carpets—with some good rugs—and huge white sofas. Some glass tables. Then there are the antiques. French things, mostly. Big gilt mirrors, and a lot of that inlaid furniture with brass railings. And some Bartolozzi prints and those wishy-washy watercolours of ducal residences by his chum. And 'the Dufy'. And my three pictures." Bettina laughed. "I always feel they look distinctly ill at ease there. I often wonder if he only puts them up when I come to see him."

"Shit! So he could have lent me the money." Delia took a swig of brandy. "Then all the stuff about 'That's what friends are for,' when I apologized for asking, was just what I'd thought until today—sheer hypocrisy."

"Is that what he said?"

"Yeah. 'That's what friends are for.'"

"Mmm," said Bettina.

Delia said, "I just can't understand it. I don't mean his refusing me the loan, and so on. What I can't understand is the way he behaved this morning. Saying we were friends. Really friends. Old friends. Why—shit, man!—there were tears in his eyes when he said that. And when I saw he was actually *crying*, of course I felt I'd been wrong about him all along, and I said everything was all right—I meant it, too. And he seemed pleased, really pleased. In fact he insisted that we celebrate."

"Celebrate?"

"Yeah. Celebrate that we were friends. He said he felt that a cloud between us had blown away."

"Goodness!"

"So he insisted that we should have champagne."

"Oh, come now, Dee-dee. *He* insisted?"

"Yeah. So that we could celebrate. Shit! And when I was doubtful—you know why—he said champagne was special, that it was a tonic. He said a doctor had prescribed it for his mother. And I'd been so fucking tense, I felt I'd like a bit of a tonic. So I said, 'All right', and he fetched a new bottle, and opened it—"

"What happened to the old bottle?"

"Oh, he'd cleared that away. I suppose it had gone flat, what was left. Why are you giving me that funny look? I'm telling you exactly what happened. And he came back with the new bottle, and opened it—pop! And we drank a toast. Shit! We drank to friendship."

"You say the champagne was entirely his idea?"

"*Yeah*. I *told* you. And I felt so happy, and he was so nice. Really he was. But then at lunch-time, he started *getting at me* again. And, afterwards, he was really horrible —when I was talking about my childhood. You weren't there. But he was even worse, later—surely you remember?"

"He *lied* to me," said Bettina. She sounded incredulous.

"What?" Delia sounded puzzled.

"Deliberately lied. Deliberately. To *me*."

"What?" Delia looked owlish.

"Oh, forget it. It's nothing. What were you saying, Dee-dee?"

"You know—that I couldn't understand why he was so nice, and then started being horrible again, so horrible, such a short time later. Shit!"

"Mission accomplished! No, I don't suppose you could understand, Dee-dee."

"How d'you mean—'mission accomplished'?"

"Oh, I don't know." Bettina laughed. "Perhaps I'm a bit drunk. What was that you called him? 'Old snaky'?" Bettina was laughing as Johnny came out of the front door.

He said, "You sound very merry."

"Yes, indeed," said Bettina. "Merry as a grig."

"What *is* a grig? I've never known. A kind of dance, d'you think?" he asked. "Something like a jig?"

Bettina said, "It's a kind of cricket, I believe."

"I've heard of *French* cricket. . . ."

"Not that sort of cricket. A grasshopper."

"Oh, *that* kind of cricket, scraping away with sheer *joie de vivre*." He sat down, and looked at Bettina. After a moment he said, "Why are you scanning me with those X-ray eyes? It's rather intimidating. Are you trying to read me like a glove?"

"A *book*," said Delia.

"Nonsense," said Johnny. "You're thinking of, 'If the book fits, wear it'."

Delia was frowning, swaying her head a little. "But—"

"He's joking, Dee-dee."

"Oh."

Johnny lit a cigarette. Bettina said, "Give me one of those."

"Darling, of course. Or shall I fetch your packet of Disque Bleu, wherever it is?"

"No, one of those will do." She took one, and Johnny lit it.

"Your fourth," said Delia. She started counting on her fingers. "One after breakfast. One in the middle of the morning. One after lunch. One before dinner—that's this one."

"In the cocktail hour," said Johnny, with a glance at Delia's glass. He raised his eyebrows. He looked towards Bettina, but she was staring straight ahead.

Delia said, "And one after dinner. That makes five."

Johnny clapped. "Our little mathematician! Well, perhaps not exactly *little*. . . ." Again he looked at Bettina's profile.

"Shit, Johnny, why do you wear those dark glasses at night?" said Delia. "It's weird."

He said, "They relax my eyes." Delia drank some brandy. Bettina went on staring towards the invisible rocks. Her cigarette was in her right hand; with her left, she fingered her crab pendant. The muscle by Johnny's mouth twitched once, then twitched again.

Delia put down her glass. Now her frown was thoughtful, rather than puzzled. She frowned down into her drink. Then she rested her elbows on the table—one of them skidded, and she pulled it back—and put her chin between the cupped palms of her hands. Still frowning, she raised her head and began to gaze at Johnny. After a moment, he stubbed out his cigarette. She went on gazing. He seemed about to speak when, suddenly, she said, "Mission accomplished!" Then, "Oh!" Then, "I'm going to hurl cats." She leapt up and ran into the house, heels clacking.

"*Hurl cats*?" said Bettina.

"It's a dreadful South African slang expression for vomiting." Johnny laughed.

"Oh, I see." Bettina still stared ahead, face impassive.

"Mission accomplished?" said Johnny. "What on earth did she mean by that?"

"Don't ask *me*."

"I suppose she's gone haywire after all that booze that she's throwing up."

Although Bettina had only taken a few puffs at her cigarette, she now stubbed it out. Then she said, "Johnny."

"Yes, darling."

"Tomorrow's Monday. There's a flight to London at half-past eleven. I'm sure we'll be able to get you on it. The season's over, and we'll go to the airport early."

Johnny's mouth had opened while she was speaking. Now it stayed open as he looked at her blankly. Then he said, "You want me to *leave*?"

"Yes."

"You want me to leave *tomorrow*?"

"Yes."

He gave a puzzled laugh. He said, "Darling, this is so sudden!" Then, "It's because of *her*, isn't it?"

"In a way."

"Darling, if I promise, really promise to be good?"

His charm, like his cigarette smoke, hovered in the air.

"No, Johnny."

"Awfully, awfully good."

"No."

There was a pause. Then he said, "But won't it be rather awful for you, darling, all alone with her here, when she's on a *binge*?"

"I shall manage."

There was another pause. He said, "She's only here for another six days. I could stay at that hotel in the town—the one where we had drinkies last week—till she goes, and then come nipping back here with you, in the car, after you've driven her to the airport." Then, "We'd have champagne. To celebrate."

"*No.*" The voice—icy, stressed—in which she said this made him flinch.

"Bettina. . . ."

The low rolling sound came from the distance. They both ignored it.

"No." Her tone was normal again.

"All right, darling. Well, if you insist . . . of course I must go . . . have to go . . . I see. . . . Shall I come back next month, when it's getting cold? I'll light a fire in the hall every evening. I make very good fires, as you know. Boy Scout training, and all that. We'll have rum toddies and we'll have *fondue*. No reason why one should have fondue only in Switzerland. Those boring people don't deserve a monopoly of anything. They've achieved nothing but the cuckoo-clock, as Harry Lime said in *The Third Man*. I loved that film, especially Harry. He had such charm."

Bettina said, "He was a murderer."

"I always forget that part. But will it be all right? About next month? I'll put off looking for a new job a bit longer."

"No, don't do that."

"Anyway, you'll be in London sometime soon, won't you?"

"No, I'm staying here."

"All winter?"

She nodded.

"For Christmas? Christmas might be fun. Perhaps I could put off my mama till New Year—just this once. I'll bring you a gorgeous hamper from Fortnum's. Or would you prefer Harrods?"

She said, "Johnny, I don't want you to come back."

"What?" he said. Then he said, "Never?" He laughed as if she had been joking. He said, "Wot, never no more?"

"Never."

It was a spasm that grappled his face now. He wrestled free. "Bettina, darling Bettina, *why*?"

She said nothing. Her look at him was steady and serene; it was unperturbed. He stood up. "Tomorrow then," he said. He went into the house. Bettina smoothed her smooth hair. Then she took a sip of wine.

Delia came out on to the terrace. "Sorry about that," she said. Then, "Where's Johnny?"

"Oh, he went to his room."

"Oh?" Then again she said, "I'm sorry. Shit! You see I suddenly worked out what you meant by 'mission accomplished'. That he wanted to start me drinking again. That was what it was all about: all the charm, and the being friends, and so on. That was what you meant, wasn't it? Then he could start being horrible to me again. Shit! But *why*?"

"Who knows?"

Delia picked up her drink, and finished it, standing. "Shit!—I need a drink," she said taking her glass over to the trolley.

"How about something to eat?"

"Some of Johnny's *exquisite* little sandwiches? I feel they might be poisoned. But of course he didn't make them just for me. Anyway, I'm not hungry." With her small tumbler three-quarters full of brandy, she came back to the table, and sat down.

"So you still feel like drinking?"

"You mean that now I know what Johnny was up to, I should feel put off? Shit!—things don't work out like that. Anyway, I'm having a good time. Or shall be, as soon as I forget about old snaky. It's great to have a drink again. And, after all, I *am* on holiday."

"I only thought that you might feel squeamish. Just after *hurling cats*."

Delia laughed. "Shit! That certainly sounds funny when *you* say it. Why haven't you got one, by the way? A cat, I mean. You've always had a cat."

"I was very tempted by a small one in the town the other day. Black, except for a blaze on its forehead. Very thin. But it was wild. It ran away. Just as well."

"Why just as well?"

"Oh, who'd look after it when I'm not here." Then she laughed. "When a woman asks me to look at her new baby, I always wish it were a kitten. Then I could show some genuine enthusiasm."

"You've never been keen on babies, have you?"

"No, never. I've always been amazed by the way some women peer into strange prams."

Delia laughed. "Shit!—you make it sound obscene. But

I've never been that keen myself. In general. Only on Eleanor."

"You still miss her?"

"Yeah. Oh, yeah. It's not sort of . . . an open wound, like it used to be. But it's as if a part of me were missing. I've heard people say that they feel pain in missing limbs. Particularly when it rains. And of course it always rains in England." Delia gave her loud laugh.

"I was wondering if we could have her kidnapped."

"*Kidnapped*? Shit, Bettina—what an idea! Not like you at all."

"*Not like me*? Why—*not like me*?"

"I've never heard you sound so angry. Shit!—don't be angry with me. I just meant that the idea's . . . well, so wild."

"So wild. *Not like me*." In a pause, Delia stared at Bettina with a puzzled frown, head swaying a little, eyes slightly glazed. When Bettina spoke again, her tone was calm, brisk. "I've been thinking a lot about you and Eleanor recently. I feel sure it would be possible to have her kidnapped."

"Too late."

"Too late?"

"Oh, yeah. Yeah! I don't know if she hates me, but I'm sure she doesn't love me. She was only two when I left. I'm certain she's been completely brainwashed by my mom and dad. By her father."

"I should have thought of it years ago." Then, "Would you have taken it—that *African* money."

"Perhaps I would have. For Eleanor. I don't know." Then, "Perhaps you should simply have arranged it, without asking me." And the loud laugh.

"Like a *deus ex machina*?"

"A god from a machine. Shit!—I've never known exactly what that means. Or perhaps I've forgotten. Perhaps I knew at varsity."

"In the ancient Greek theatre, there were machines they used when a god had to interfere at the appropriate moment. Like the chariot drawn by dragons that came to rescue Medea, when Jason was going to kill her."

"Why did it come to rescue her? She'd murdered her children."

"She had to. She loved them. But it was a question of honour."

"Shit—Bettina!"

"Anyway, let's not argue about that. The point is that I should have done the equivalent of appearing in a chariot to rescue Eleanor ten years ago. I see that now."

"It's nice of you to think of it. Very, very nice. Shit!—I really appreciate it." As she took a mouthful of her drink, tears came into Delia's eyes, and she snuffled. "Very, very nice," she repeated.

"Nice? Not nice at all. It's academic now. I thought of it too late. I've wasted so much time. On what I thought was an art of living, but now I see was only a game. Travelling. Doing up houses. Entertaining. All that business about clothes that you were deploring earlier."

"Deploring? Shit!—I wasn't deploring it for *you*. Just saying that it couldn't ever have been a thing of *mine*. But I've always thought your clothes were lovely. I remember once sitting talking to you while you were packing, and there were all those romantic underclothes piled on the bed. Satin and very fine cotton and real silk—shit!"

"I've always detested synthetic materials."

"And such colours! Deep rose and violet and sea-green. And a set of things with a pattern like cream swirled onto blackberries. And there were white ones too. I remember a broderie-anglaise nightdress. In among the embroidery, there were tiny forget-me-nots. Shit!—just the same blue as your eyes."

"Goodness, how extraordinary that you should remember all that. Yes, I've always been fond of underclothes. Undressing. In the afternoon—white linen sheets in a room with a thin blue blind. Or at night—in a dark studio with one little red-shaded lamp. Art of love, I thought, as well as art of living. *Game* of living, *game* of love."

"Oh. . . ." Delia was looking perplexed.

"Yes, fond of underclothes. Dresses, too. An unbroken line. Trousers, sometimes, with a long tunic. But never skirts or shirts or suits."

"Little Chanel suits."

Bettina laughed. "Especially not those!"

Delia said, "Did you marry Max to get away from home?"

"Partly. But only partly. He attracted me, too. At that stage a father-figure was exactly what I needed. And I'd realized that the ballet wasn't going to work out. And the idea of a strange country was attractive. Even *that* country!"

Delia sighed, then said in a dreamy voice, "Even that one!"

"And of course the money was alluring. Yes, indeed! Money and good looks have been my ruin." Bettina laughed. "Money and beauty. Possessions and lovers. Eating lovers. Lovers are like grapes." She raised her face and her right hand, cupped, palm upwards, towards the hanging purple bunches. "These tasteless ones are appropriate. After the pleasure's over, lovers become tasteless."

"You found that lovers were . . . a great pleasure?" Delia had finished her drink. Now she stood up, and went over to the trolley.

"Oh yes, a very great pleasure. One of my great distractions."

Delia, pouring brandy, said, "You don't find . . . getting there . . . difficult?" She spoke tentatively, with delicacy.

"*Getting there*? Oh, I see. No, hardly ever. Of course I've always chosen my lovers carefully. Just as I chose the objects that I bought with money. And I could always buy good lovers with my beauty."

Delia came back to the table. Her face, already flushed with drink, was now a deep red. Sitting down, not looking at Bettina, she said, "Never a thing of mine. Getting there. Sometimes I make jokes about it. Shit! Like I did this morning when I said I preferred a good dinner. But that's true, of course. I . . . can't. . . ."

"Can't 'get there'?"

"Not at all."

"Never? Nothing with Ellis?"

"Shit!—no. Nothing at all. It wasn't so bad, to begin with, when I was in love with him—"

Bettina laughed. "Ah! 'In love!' Now *that*'s not one of *my* things."

"Oh! Anyway, I could put up with it, when I was in love. But then I used to have to get drunk to make it bearable. Ever since, before I go to bed with anyone, I have to get drunk."

"A lot of drink certainly wouldn't help. Except as an

anaesthetic." Bettina paused. Then she said, "Perhaps you're lucky."

"Shit! You can't believe that."

"Perhaps I can believe it more than you can. Lovers. Grapes. Tasteless. You spit out the pips and the skin. *Wasting time*. Distracting me from doing what I wanted. From painting."

Delia took a drink. She had stopped blushing. She said, "Shit—but you *did* paint!"

"Yes, I painted. But not as I should have. Single-mindedly. All those arty games of love and living got in the way. It was my own fault. I made wrong choices."

"But it's not too late. You're not old. You can start painting again. You can devote yourself to it. And—shit!—it's not as if you were a beginner."

"Mmm. There's a poem of Rilke's I used to recite to myself. I think I can still recite it. Shall I recite it to you now?"

"Yeah," Delia said, "Yeah, sure."

> *"A god has power. But can a mere man follow*
> *The Lyre's subtle music? Out of joint*
> *His senses are. And at the crossing-point*
> *Of heart-ways stands no Temple of Apollo.*
>
>
> *Singing, you'll soon find out, is not desire,*
> *Not courting of things easily attained.*
> *Singing is being—for the god, unstrained—*
> *But how for us? And when shall he require*
> *That we to earth and to the stars return?*

Young man, it is not when with first-love seething
A voice mounts passionately to the closed mouth. Learn
To forget you sang. It was of no avail.
True song demands a different kind of breathing.
A calm. A shudder in the god. A gale."

Delia drank. "Yeah," she said. "Yeah, Shit!—that's terrific. *Wonderful*," she effused. And then, "You see!"

"See what?"

"Oh, shit, that you needn't be young to do things. In fact, it's actually a good thing to be older."

"You think *that*'s the poem's message? Hmm. Anyway, it *is* too late. You'll just have to take my word for that, Dee-dee."

"Beauty and money," Delia said. "Your ruin, you say? I've never had either. Never wanted either. Not really."

"Well, Dee-dee, you're going to have to face up to having money. I've left you a lot of it. In my will."

"Your *will*! Oh, shit, Bettina, don't be silly. You're only two years older than me. And you take much better care of yourself. You'll outlive me by years."

"Let's not go into all that. The point is that I've made the bequest. I didn't arrange that kidnapping, as I should have, all those years ago, so surely I can leave you some money, to do whatever you want with, *now*."

"But Bettina, dearest Bettina"—Delia gulped from her glass—"you know I couldn't take it."

"*African* money—oh, I know all that. But the money will be yours with no provisos. If you want to, you can give it all to *the cause*, as Johnny calls it."

"Wonder where he's got to."

"Oh, he's in his room. He's probably in an odd mood."

Bettina took a sip of wine. "As a matter of fact, he has decided to leave tomorrow."

"To leave? Shit—that's because of me, isn't it?"

"No, it isn't."

"Oh I'm sure it must be."

"I promise it isn't."

"*Really* promise?"

"What a child you are. Yes, *really* promise. He's just restless. You know what Johnny's like."

Delia laughed. "Do I? Shit, I'm sure I *don't*. Anyway, what I wanted to say is that it's just silly, this talking about your will."

"You've already said that."

"Yeah. And I'll say it again. It's just silly."

"You can give it all away if you want to. But there's one thing I wish you'd do. Use a little of it to buy yourself a house or flat."

"Shit—a house? A flat?"

"Yes, get out of that attic in your friends' house, and buy a little place of your own."

Delia drank some brandy. "A place of my own!" She wore a bemused look. Now her voice lowered. "Not a house. I wouldn't want a house. What would I do with a house? Shit!—I suppose I could have people to stay. Refugees from back home. There are so many of them with nowhere to go. Yet I do like having a bolt-hole of my own. I feel guilty about that, of course. But I see people all day, and I like to scramble into my little burrow at night. And I'd have to organize them all, and the electricity bills, and so on. I organize all day at work, so I wouldn't want to organize at home, as well. Selfish—shit! But there you are. I wouldn't want a house. But a flat. . . ." She drank again. "Do you know Highbury Fields?"

"No. Is it in North London? I don't know North London very well." Delia nodded. Bettina said, "Wasn't it one of those places you said made you feel afraid?"

"Highbury Fields? No! Oh no, never. That was Highbury New Park. Highbury New Park isn't a park at all. It's just a creepy street. Highbury Fields is a park, in a way, but it doesn't have railings. There's a swimming-pool—shit! Imagine swimming in England!—and a children's playground at the bottom. But further on, there's just the grass and these big plane trees. Whenever—ha ha!—there's a fine day, people lie on the grass with their shirts off—you know the way the English do. And dogs bound about and chase each other. You wouldn't like *that*, but they look joyful, somehow. And overlooking the Fields, there's this terrace of houses. Plain old brick houses. Georgian, I suppose—yeah, they'd be Georgian. Sash windows, and fan-lights over the doors. Those houses are almost all made into flats. Two-room flats—one on each floor. I've often thought that the place I'd most like to live—in England I mean, till I go back home—is in one of those flats. On the top floor, looking out into the branches of those plane trees. The tube station's just down at the bottom of the road, yet the road's so quiet. And there's this feeling of space. The Fields are wide. Although there's a crescent of houses—big detached houses—on the other side, they seem a long way off. Anyway, in summer, the plane trees hide them. And up at the top of the road, where the Fields end, there are these great chestnuts, with the heavy white blossoms—they're like little towers. Shit! You know, sometimes, on a Sunday afternoon, when I'm feeling a bit down, and the Zimmermanns' kids are making a helluva noise, I walk down the Holloway Road, and just wander round Highbury Fields." Delia paused. "It's gentrified, of course. But it's not all *that* posh, because the flats aren't big enough. And the MP is Labour, and so's the local council. Shit!—I could never live in an area that voted Tory. It would give me the creeps." She laughed loudly. "Yeah, it would give me the creeps to live among creeps!" Her voice lowered again. "I suppose I've always thought Highbury Fields is the best of two worlds. Having your cake and eating it. Yeah. . . ."

"Well, you could get a flat there."

"Shit—you must be joking! They're helluva pricey. Like everything in London. There used to be decent days when you could rent flats—quite cheaply, too. But not any more. Now you've got to buy. Everyone's tied up with mortgages. All they think about is the fucking mortgage."

"Of course, for tax purposes, it's absurd not to have a mortgage. But one *can* pay cash."

"It's all a crazy dream—shit! Living by Highbury Fields. And, Bettina, I was never meant to own property. That's how they trap you. As soon as you own property, you change. You've joined the other side."

"Oh, Dee-dee, what absolute *nonsense*. Lots of socialists —communists, too—own their houses."

"Yeah, I know, and I'm not blaming them. Shit!—they have to buy, because there's nothing to rent, and they've got kids, and so on. They can't just live in a room, like I do. *But I can.* Oh, I know you don't like my room. I could see you didn't that time when you came to the house to fetch me. You asked why I had that big hideous desk, taking up so much space, and why didn't I get a table instead. And why did I have those stacks of old pamphlets. 'You obviously never consult them. They're thick with dust.' That was what you said."

"How rude of me! Did I really say that? I don't remember."

"Yeah. The only thing you liked was Jake's picture. Though you said one of the posters was quite a good design. But I could see you frowning at the Sellotape—it always peels off. You asked why I didn't get that poster framed."

"I'm sorry, Dee-dee. I—"

"Shit!—don't apologize. I know all that sort of thing means a lot to you. And if I had my own place, I'd probably take more trouble. No, I'm not contradicting myself. I don't think I *ought* to take all that much trouble, you see. Though I'd like one of your paintings." She paused. "Shit! Johnny has three."

"As I told you, Dee-dee, I never knew you wanted one. One doesn't press one's work on people, uninvited. Johnny *asked* for his."

"Oh, well. Anyway, one of your pictures would probably make my old desk and the heaps of pamphlets and the wardrobe with the suitcases on top look even worse, by contrast. Jake's picture is different. Been a part of my life for so long. But *all* those things, Bettina— the desk and pamphlets, and so on—are parts of my life."

After a moment, Bettina said, "Yes I understand that. I'm sorry."

"Don't be." Delia smiled. Suddenly she stretched out her hand, and with her forefinger stroked Bettina's right eyebrow. "Lovely," she said. "Shit! Like a wing. Or do I mean a feather? A raven's feather, like Balzac used to write with."

Laughing, Bettina gently put Delia's hand back on the table. "Remember—it's a fake. If you touch it, the black comes off." Then, "Think about that flat by Highbury Fields."

"*Think*? Shit!—dream, you mean. And thank God it is only a dream, if I had to buy it with money you'd *left* me. You and your *will*, Bettina!" Delia, shaking her head, laughed with affection. "What's that poem?" she said. "Of Browning's? Oh yeah—'The Bishop Orders his Tomb'."

Bettina closed her eyes. Then she opened them, and said, "I haven't gone to quite those lengths. A *tomb* really sounds rather bizarre, nowadays. Though I've always thought it would be rather fun to be sculpted on one, like a Norman. Except that I'd have a cat instead of a dog at my feet. But what would one wear? I suppose a kaftan would do as well as anything. The folds would be a treat for the monumental mason. I wonder if monumental masons still exist. Anyway, interesting monuments aren't allowed any more. How boring all those delicious country church-yards would be if the clergy had felt that way in the past. Nothing but grim, flat slabs—usually a dreadful sort of pinky brown, or grey—and squat square crosses. Not even eccentric inscriptions are permitted. All so dreary. It's probably intended to encourage cremation. Anyway, cremation's what I've chosen. The thing is, Dee-dee, that I'm going to die soon."

Delia had been listening to this monologue with a somewhat glassy look. Bettina had spoken the last sentence in the same tone as the rest. Now Delia took a gulp of brandy. Then she said, "*What* did you say?"

"Don't hedge, Dee-dee. You heard me perfectly well."

"But you can't *mean* it?"

"Of course, I *mean* it. Why should I invent something so drab? Anyway, it would be in the worst possible taste."

"But. . . ."

Bettina lifted up her pendant, shook it in the air, then replaced it. "My sign, you know. Cancer. Cancer of the ovaries. Haven't you noticed my great big belly?" Leaning back, Bettina smoothed her hand down over her stomach. She looked down at its roundness, then, with a small grimace, pulled the folds of the kaftan loose again.

"No," said Delia. "Shit! No!" Tears had filled her eyes, and now rolled down her cheeks. She pushed at them with her hand. "But you should be having treatment. You should be in hospital."

"No, Dee-dee. I've only got a few months. I made the doctor tell me. He started talking about chemotherapy, but in the end he admitted that it was too late, even for that. Having it would just be going through the motions. And what motions! Vomiting. One's hair falling out." She smoothed it. "Not being able to have a bath because one comes out in blisters. Dreadful depression, too. I suppose I could have faced all that, if there were a chance. But they admit there isn't. So I've decided that I want to die with dignity."

After a moment, Delia said, "You'll be coming back to England?"

"No, I don't want to die in a nursing-home. I've decided to stay here."

"Stay here? But you haven't even got a telephone."

"Thank heaven! Doctors and people tracking me down. Gloomy chats. But I've made an arrangement. With a taxi-driver in the town. When I don't have visitors, he drives out here every morning at nine. I pay him extraordinarily well, and he never misses—I've told him that, if he ever does, the arrangement's over, though he can send his brother if he needs a day off. I've told him I have a weak heart, and I want to be on the safe side. He parks up there"—she gestured towards the hillside—"where I leave my car, you know, and hoots his horn. Then he comes down the track, till he can see the house, and I wave from the terrace. If, one day, I didn't do it, he'd come to investigate. And then . . . then he'd go and tell a lawyer in the town who has a letter of instructions. About telephoning my lawyer in England, flying my body back, to be cremated, and so on."

"But, shit!—you may not die. Just like that. You may be in pain."

"Oh, no. I've worked out all that. Of course, the pain is going to become much worse. At the moment I'm taking paracetamol. Soon, that won't be enough. The little safe in my room is full of morphine. Do you know, Dee-dee, some hospitals won't give dying patients too much morphine in case they become *addicted*?"

"Shit!"

"Yes, indeed. Anyway, when the pain gets too bad —when I become . . . its creature . . . and I realize that I'll be too weak to get up and wave to the taxi-driver next day—I shall take the really big dose of morphine. The final one."

"Shit! All alone? Dear Bettina. Not with a friend?"

"What a strain *that* would be! Watching one's chum getting glummer and glummer."

Delia said, "Have you told Johnny?"

"Johnny? Good heavens, no! What an idea! I've never had any intention of telling him. Think how embarrassed he'd be. *Awfully* embarrassed! I didn't mean to tell *you* . . . but I weakened."

"What about getting a nurse?"

"*Quel horreur*! Measuring out my doses, and trying to keep me hanging on, and calling me 'we'. 'We must try to eat a little of our nice din-dins, now.'" Bettina laughed. "'Good Bettina! Good doggie!'" She said, "I'd far rather be alone. My Garbo act, you know."

Delia was fiddling desperately with her empty glass. Now she said, "I've simply got to have a drink. Won't you have one?"

"I've still got some wine. Are you sure you don't feel like having a sandwich?"

Moving towards the trolley, Delia said, with passion, "Oh, shit—how can you talk about *sandwiches*?"

"How can *you* talk about drinks?"

"Yeah. . . ."

"Anyway, I'm not worried about your expiring from starvation. Though I do think it's a bad idea to drink without eating anything. Sandwiches can be survival. I'll have one, a little later. I intend to survive as long as I can. With dignity. Listening to Mozart. Reading my Greek plays."

Delia, pouring her drink, said, "But, Bettina—shit, doesn't it worry you that those plays are only about myths? Myths that are over and done with."

"Over and done with, you mean, in the sense that we don't worship the Greek gods? Myths in the sense that we don't literally believe them? *That* doesn't worry *me*! Of course it doesn't. Truth lives in the art." She paused. Then, "You know those rocks out there, those three rocks that we've compared to so many things?"

"Yeah," said Delia, coming back to the table, sitting, taking a mouthful of brandy, swallowing it down.

"*I* often think of them—please don't laugh! I don't mean to be pompous—as Aeschylus, Sophocles and Euripides. The three great Greek tragedians. Greek tragedy, I'll have you know, Dee-dee, is based simply on three characters and a chorus. On that basis, those tragedians developed the most truthful and terrible art. I look at those rocks, and I think of those three artists. I think of the stories, too, that I've heard about their deaths. Aeschylus, who had written so much about the pursuit of people by fate, was told by an oracle that the fall of a house would kill him. So he went out into the fields to avoid his destiny. Perhaps he hoped that, like Orestes, he would escape the Furies. But, out in the fields, an eagle, carrying a tortoise, mistook his bald head for a stone. The eagle wanted to eat the tortoise. It dropped it on the 'stone', to break its shell. So Aeschylus was killed, in accordance with the oracle, by the fall of a house. The house of a tortoise.

"Then there was Sophocles. He'd written of Antigone's extraordinary devotion to her father. His own children tried to prove him insane, in order to gain possession of his property. His defence was to read aloud his play about the death of Antigone's father, Oedipus, at Colonus. And he won his case, and lived on to be ninety. They say he died of joy at winning a poetry prize at the Olympic games—he who had such a grim view of the possibilities of human success, human happiness.

"But the strangest death of all is the death of Euripides, who wrote *The Bacchae*—the story I told you this morning about Dionysus and Pentheus and the maenads. A foreign king invited Euripides, as an honoured guest, to his court. But the king's courtiers were jealous, and they set a pack of savage dogs on him. The dogs tore Euripides to pieces. I wonder if, as he died, he thought how his Bacchae, his maenads, had done the same thing to Pentheus."

A flicker of lightning played over the surface of the sea. "There they are! The rocks! The poets! Do you see them?"

Delia's "No"—she had been wiping her hand across her

eyes again—came as the thunder rolled; closer now, but still quite far away.

Bettina said, "They're all legends, of course. The stories of those deaths. Just as the myths are. But the works aren't legends. They live—and so they keep the myths alive. Just as the Christian myths will live in art, long after everyone has stopped believing in them. I prefer the Greek myths to the Christian ones—they seem to me more true to life and death. But that's beside the point. The point is that people will know what it felt like to be Christians, as we know what it felt like to be Ancient Greeks. Your Muslim friends, Dee-dee, are going to do badly when their religion dies. No paintings, sculpture, poems, music about people who are gods and gods who are people! Just some ruined mosques and patterned artefacts among the dried-up oil-wells in the desert sand. Does that thought please you, Dee-dee?"

But Delia was sobbing. "Oh, Bettina, Bettina."

"Sssh, Dee-dee." Bettina rested a hand on Delia's shoulder. Delia at once seized the hand, and clasped it. "I don't really feel so bad about things. I haven't ordered my tomb, as the Bishop did. But, do you know, I've planned my death. Of course to do that is presumptuous. Hubristic. Perhaps I shall be struck by lightning." She smiled. "But that would be a very easy way out." She paused, then went on: "I've thought about it a lot. At one time, I thought that—just before I took that final big dose of morphine—I'd look at a reproduction of Rembrandt's last self-portrait. I'd read *Oedipus the King*. I'd listen to Mozart's Requiem—oh, he was so feverish and terrified when he composed it. Yet he wrote to a friend, 'And so I finish my death-song; I must not leave it incomplete. Life was indeed so beautiful, my career began under such

fortunate auspices; but one cannot change one's destiny.'
Did you hear that, Dee-dee?"

Delia was slumped forward over the table. "Yeah," she
said. "Yeah."

"But then, Dee-dee, I thought it would be rather pretentious of me to die in the company of such painting, such
words, such music." Bettina pulled her hand from Delia's
grasp, and straightened in her chair. She said, "So what I
decided to do is just look at my cup. My maenad cup. Shall
I show you my maenad cup, Dee-dee? It's with the morphine in my safe."

"Yeah! Shit! Yeah! Of course I want to see it." Delia
covered her face with her hands as Bettina went into the
house, carrying the tray on which were wine glasses, wine
bottle and ashtray. Then she leapt up, reeled over to the
trolley, topped up her glass, and was back at the table in a
moment, sitting in the same position as before. She looked
up as Bettina came on to the terrace.

The cup was shaped like a wide shallow chalice, and
Bettina carried it—as if it were a chalice—in both hands.
She put it down at the very centre of the table, directly
under the light.

"Oh!" As she looked, Delia's blurred eyes seemed to
clear, and her bemused expression to become intelligent.
She gazed. "Oh! The maenads!"

Bettina said, "See how this one dances in ecstasy, one
arm curved above her rippling hair, while the other is
clasped round that great flower-painted wine bowl."

"And this one brandishes a little spotted fawn in the
air."

"This one flourishes a staff, wreathed with ivy."

"The one wearing a leopard-skin has a hissing snake
wound round her head."

Bettina said, "See the soft brown of the pottery, the glossy black of the painting."

"Their dresses fall into pleats that have the rhythm of waves."

"All round the lower rim moves the pattern of their feet."

Delia said, "Treading so lightly."

"Yes, their feet hardly touch the ground. They're far beyond themselves. They are possessed by the god."

"Oh, their lightness, their lightness."

"Yes, the lightness of the maenads raising me out of time. The soft brown, the glossy black fading, merging, as sight dies from my eyes."

"*Bettina*! Shit—Bettina!" As Delia looked up from the cup, her eyes blurred.

"But don't they make you feel better, Dee-dee?"

"The maenads?" Delia looked down at the cup again. She said, "Yes, they do."

"I'm glad. And now"—Bettina, who had been standing bowed over the cup, sat down—"I want to be practical. Dee-dee, do you understand now that it wasn't a fantasy when I talked about my will?"

Delia, drinking, said nothing. Her bemused look was back.

"Delia!"

"Yeah?"

"You understand that the money will be yours to do as you like with?"

"Oh, shit! Yeah."

"You can give it to *the cause*. Not what I would have done myself. I've never cared for politics. At one time, Dee-dee, I was afraid that politics were going to desiccate you. They often dry up the poetry in people. Have you noticed that?"

Delia's nod was glum. "Yeah."

"Politics can replace art with sexless couples, stern or grinning, striding into the future with clenched fists. Have you noticed that?"

"But those days are over. All that is changing now. It's going to be quite different."

"I hope you're right. At least you believe that you are. And you *want* to be right. I was so pleased, this morning, when you talked about Balzac and his raven's feather."

"Like one of your eyebrows," Delia muttered.

"And I was pleased when you recited that poem of yours. Will you write it out for me? I'd like to have it."

"*Really*? Shit! Yeah—of course I will."

"And I was most pleased of all that you loved the maenads. That you understood them." Bettina smiled. "But I'm not leaving *them* to you. They're going to a museum."

"Of course! Shit! They belong to everyone."

"Well, let us say, Dee-dee, to everyone who visits that particular museum. You know, there was a time when I was going to leave all the money to art. But now, in a way, I can see it's appropriate that it should go back to Africa. That, in a sense, it *is* African money. I just wish you'd do one thing for me—buy that flat!"

"The flat looking out onto Highbury Fields!" Delia shook her head. She gave a deep sigh.

"But I won't blackmail you, emotionally. The decision is entirely yours. We won't talk about it again."

"No, no. Let's not. Shit—money!" Delia drained her

glass. "How can we talk about money when I'm going to miss you so, Bettina? Oh, Bettina!" She began to sob again.

Bettina said, "Dee–dee, you're dreadfully drunk, you know."

Delia wailed, "Yes, yes, I know. It's taken me over, just I told you it does. And I know I'm going to want to go on drinking. For another three days, at least. Shit!—perhaps four. But I may feel too awful on the fourth day, to drink anything. I *may*. . . ."

"Delia, we'll never meet again, you know. You've only got another week here. And I don't want you to be drunk all the time. Wasting our last time together, getting drunker and drunker."

"I know. I know. But I can't stop now. I don't know how."

Bettina said, "How long would it take you to get over the craving, if there simply wasn't anything for you to drink?"

"If there simply wasn't anything? Shit! Oh, about twenty-four hours I should think." She sobbed. "I ought to go and live in an Islamic country. In Saudi Arabia. That would be the answer."

Bettina's laugh in response to this was wholly joyful. "Fool!" She said the word in the exact affectionate tone she had earlier used to Johnny.

"Or in Iran."

"Fool!"

"If you lock the drink in cupboards, I might break them open. Shit! Or just set off for the town. On foot, if you wouldn't let me drive the car."

"I most certainly wouldn't let you!" Then Bettina said, "I could lock you up."

"Lock me up?" Head on one side, Delia stared at Bettina.

"Yes. In your room. You'd never break that door down. And, of course, I'd lock it on the outside, and take away the key. There's the wrought-iron guard over your bedroom window, and only that tiny little skylight in your bathroom. You couldn't possibly get out." Bettina laughed.

"Lock me up?" Delia repeated. "Shit! As if I were in jail."

"That's right." Bettina laughed again. "I'd bring you food, of course. If you were savage and raving, I needn't even open the door. I could push it through the window-guard. Like feeding animals at the zoo."

This made Delia smile. "Oh, I wouldn't *attack* you, or anything like that. Shit!"

"I'm glad to hear it. I just have to run Johnny into town in the morning. Otherwise I'll be here with you. We'll chat through the window, like Romeo and Juliet." She laughed. "Dee-dee, I think I *am* going to blackmail you emotionally about this. And then I'll be a *deus*—or, rather, *dea—ex machina*. I'd so much like you to be sober."

"Yeah. Shit!—I understand that. But I feel frightened."

"Do it for me."

Delia finished her drink. She said, "Yeah—I'll do it."

"Let's go now, then."

"Now? Shit!" Delia sounded dismayed.

"Yes, I'm afraid I'm tired again. It's one of the symptoms, you see. I have to take these little rests all the time. And I need some paracetamol. I hope it works. It's starting not to."

"Yeah. I see. All right. Can I have just one more drink, to take with me?"

"Yes. If you must. How about those sandwiches?"

"Shit, no."

"Well, if you feel hungry, later in the night. I'll bring you some. In a few hours, I'm sure to be wandering about out here. I'm always restless, a bit later."

Lightning quivered. Thunder rolled. "The Queen of the Night," said Delia.

"Still some way off," said Bettina. "But we're definitely going to have a storm."

"Rain. The country needs rain." Delia nodded earnestly several times.

"Yes, that's right. Shall I fetch your drink?"

"Shit, no! I'll fetch it." Delia stood up, and blundered over to the trolley. She filled her glass. On the way back, she tottered.

"Steady, Dee-dee," said Bettina, standing up.

Reaching Bettina, Delia put an arm round her shoulders. She leant on her heavily, and Bettina was almost forced down, but with a great effort, straightened her shoulders. "Oh, Bettina," Delia mumbled, as they went indoors.

Light shone down on the maenad cup. Then the dimmer rectangle of light came on behind Delia's window-guard. Several minutes passed. Then the light went out. A moment later came the sound of a turned key. Then Bettina—now she was stooping, like an old woman—passed the door, without looking out. She switched off the terrace lamp, and, a moment later, the light went out in the hall. Darkness on the terrace was complete, except that, under the table, the tiny snake's eye of the insect-coil still glowed.

NIGHT

Lightning flickered: a drunkard was circling the horizon with a flashlight. Thunder echoed: a madman grumbled in a distant cave. On the terrace, the insect-coil still glowed. A sound of snoring came from Delia's room.

Now the lamp above the table was switched on; it lit the maenad cup, and made its black interior glisten. Johnny emerged from the house, from the shadows. He was carrying his bag. He wore a vertiginously pink kaftan, and he had shaved off his moustache. He was not wearing his dark glasses. His eyes looked large; the pupils were tiny.

He sat down in Bettina's chair. Putting his bag on his lap, he unzipped it, and started to unpack its contents. First he took out his cigarettes and lighter, and lit a cigarette. Next he unfolded a metal-rimmed shaving-mirror, and stood it on the table. Round it he arranged a can of hair-spray, an atomizer of scent, and various items of make-up. Behind these, he placed three small bottles, spacing and aligning them precisely. In one were pink tablets, in the second capsules filled with grains like children's party-cake decorations. The third bottle held a white powder.

Johnny had paid no attention to the maenad cup. Now, leaning forward, he casually flicked ash into it. Then, putting his bag on the floor, he stood up. Walking on the balls of his bare feet, he went to the drinks trolley, poured vodka into a large glass, and added tonic. He lifted the lid of the ice-bucket, replaced it, frowning. Now he raised the bottle of Rémy Martin to the light. It was two-thirds empty. He laughed; the sound was more like panting than laughter. He replaced the bottle, and went back to the table with his drink.

Sitting down, he helped himself to two pink tablets and one capsule, fastening the bottles and replacing them in their former positions. He put the three pills in his mouth, and washed them down with vodka and tonic. Then he reached for the atomizer. He sprayed scent on his wrists, behind his ears, and inside the V neck of his kaftan. "*Bain de Champagne*," he said, enunciating each syllable precisely, and stubbed out his cigarette in the maenad cup.

Now he adjusted the angle of the mirror. He shook a bottle of cream-coloured lotion before putting dabs of it all over his face, and then blending them together. His face was now a pale mask; it became still paler when he coated it with ivory powder. Next he applied pink lipstick, then darkened his eyelashes with mascara, and covered his eyelids with blue shadow. Using a soft pencil he superimposed black arches on his own eyebrows. Finally, he parted his hair in the centre, smoothed it back, and fixed it in place with a blast of hair-spray. He gazed fondly at his face in the mirror. "Darling," he said, and then, softly, "Fool!"

The sound of snores from Delia's room had stopped. Now she called, "Bettina!"

He answered, "Yes, Dee-dee."

"*Bettina?*"

The puzzled tone in which Delia reiterated the name made Johnny start as if from a trance. He began to bundle his things back into his bag.

"*Bettina!*" Delia's voice was very loud.

He said, "It's not Bettina. It's . . . Johnny." Now he had scrambled everything into the bag.

Delia said, "Oh God, I want a drink. Shit! I need a drink so badly."

Getting up, he said, "Well, why not have one? I'm going to my room now, but the drinks trolley's out here. You can help yourself."

He had reached the door when Delia called out, "I *can't* help myself. I'm locked in."

He stopped. "What on earth do you mean—*locked in*?"

"Shit!—just what I say. Bettina locked me in."

"*Bettina* did?"

"Yeah. I wanted her to do it. To stop me drinking. But oh, I need a drink so terribly badly now. Just one."

Putting his bag down on the floor, Johnny gave his panting laugh. He glanced towards the trolley, but then hurried into the house. There was a bright flash of lightning. The thunder rolled as, a few moments later, he reappeared, peeling the foil off a new bottle of brandy. Close to the wall, he sidled behind the trailing vine to Delia's window. He pushed the bottle into one of the wrought-iron loops in the window-guard where it rested, as in a wine-rack. Delia was sobbing.

"Delia!" Johnny called. Her light came on, and Johnny retreated behind the curtain of vines. "I've put a bottle of brandy in your window-guard," he said. "It's Courvoisier this time, but I'm sure you'll enjoy it just as much as the Rémy Martin." Once more he panted with laughter. "Just call me St Bernard," he said. "Woof, woof." He picked up his bag and went back to the table. He sat down again in Bettina's chair.

Delia's shadow appeared. She lifted the edge of her curtain, and peered through the wrought iron. "Shit,

Johnny, where are you?" she called. Then she saw the bottle, pulled it inside, and dropped the curtain. Her shadow disappeared.

It was at that moment that the maenad cup caught Johnny's attention for the first time. He picked it up and turned it between his hands. He examined the painted figures. He frowned. "Ugh," he said with a small shiver of disgust. Putting the cup down, he stood up, and returned to his position near Delia's window. "Delia," he called.

"Yeah." Her tone was flat.

"What's that thing on the table?"

"Thing?"

"A sort of cup with horrible women on it."

"*Horrible*? Shit, they aren't *horrible*. They're marvellous. They're maenads. You know. Like Bettina was telling us about this morning."

"The ones who tore that king to pieces?"

"Yeah."

"Horrible!"

"They're beautiful. The cup is beautiful. It's Bettina's most precious possession. It. . . . She. . . ." Delia stopped. Then she said, "It means more to her than anything else in the world."

"How perfectly extraordinary," said Johnny. He returned to the table, sat down, and leant sideways, to fumble in his bag. He pulled out one of the small bottles. It was the one holding pink tablets, and he frowned and put it back. He fumbled in the bag again. This time he pulled out the bottle of white powder, and smiled. He unscrewed the cap, and poured some of the powder into the palm of his hand. He hesitated, then poured more. He tipped the powder into his mouth, and quickly picked up his glass and drank. He closed the bottle, and put it back in his bag.

Now, leaning on his elbow, blue-shadowed lids lowered, he studied the maenad cup. With his right hand, he slowly revolved it. "Ugh," he said again.

Delia's shadow reappeared on the curtain. "Johnny," she called.

He turned his head. "Yes?"

"Come here."

He sighed, but stood up and returned to his place behind the vine.

Delia said, "Where are you? I want you to take away that bottle of brandy."

"Oh no," he said. "I don't think I should do *that*."

She pushed the bottle into the wrought-iron loop. She said, "I haven't touched it. I don't want it. Please take it away."

"You may need it later."

"I won't. Shit, Johnny, *take* it."

"Delia," Johnny said.

"Yeah?" Then, "Where *are* you?"

"Just tell me something. Those women on that cup. One of them has a snake wound round her head. Why?"

"Maenads are at home with all wild creatures. Snakes included."

"How disgusting. Perfectly revolting."

Delia said, "Johnny, take away that bottle."

Lightning flashed.

"Not a chance!" Johnny gave a high giggle.

Silence was followed by a drum-roll of thunder. Then Delia said, "I'm surprised that—feeling the way you do about snakes—you're able to stay here."

"What on earth do you mean?"

"Why, this island is famous for its snakes." Delia's voice had taken on a dreamy tone.

"What nonsense!" said Johnny, but he stiffened against the wall.

"Famous for its snakes," Delia repeated. "Why, Bettina has seen four—no it was five, I think—actually on the terrace."

He said, "She would have told me."

"No, no," crooned Delia. "No, of course she wouldn't. She wouldn't have wanted to worry you. She knows you have a horror of them."

"Nonsense!" He sounded shrill. "Look how she told that story, this evening, about that writer, sliming his prey."

"That's different, Johnny," said Delia gently. "These are *real* snakes."

"I don't believe you." He began to tremble.

"Some of them are very lo-o-ong, and beige, with a darker criss-cross pattern on their skin." Delia sounded rapt; she sounded like a priestess. "They rear up till they're almost as tall as a person. They stick out their little forked tongues, and hiss. Sssss." She paused. "Others are black and shiny. They glide along so fast that they seem to ooze. They're so shiny that they look . . . slimy."

"Shut up." But he seemed fixed to the wall.

"Johnny, I'm only *telling* you. You shouldn't be annoyed. I must just warn you about the most dangerous ones of all. They're so tiny and pale, that you wouldn't even notice one on the terrace. They're deadly." She paused. Then her tone changed. Briskly, she said, "Really, it's a good thing you're leaving tomorrow. It's not likely that you'll come across any snakes tonight. Although one might want to take shelter on the terrace from the storm. It might slither up the steps: a big brown one, rearing and hissing, or an oozy black one, or a little pale one that could wriggle onto your foot."

"Shut up, bitch." Johnny, back to the wall, edged towards the door. His eyes were stretched wide. Then, with extreme caution, trembling, and gazing at the ground before every step, he moved forward, towards his bag, and reached for its handle. But then he staggered, put a hand to his forehead, sank down in Bettina's chair. "Bettina," he murmured. Then a shudder convulsed him. His eyes were fixed on the cup, on the ecstatic maenad with the snake twined round her serpent hair.

"Bettina!" he cried out. He stood up. Snatching the cup, he raised it above his head, and hurled it towards the terrace rail. It shattered on the paving. There was a flash of lightning. Johnny was stooping towards his bag when thunder crashed and the lights went out.

"Oh, my God!" Then he shouted or screamed; the sound was lost in another clap of thunder. "Its eye. Under the table. The snake's eye." He snatched up his bag. "They're after me," he cried. He ran across the terrace, down the steps, stumbling over the pebble beach to the sea, which was no longer calm: a strong wind was rising.

A moment or two later, Delia called out, "Shit! Johnny!" After that, the only sound was the rising wind.

Bettina came out of the house with a torch. She was wearing a pure white kaftan. She went to Delia's window. "Dee-dee," she called. Delia pulled back the curtain and looked out.

"Oh, Bettina. Shit! Am I glad you've come! It was creepy when the lights went out."

Bettina said, "I may be able to get them going again. I just wanted to make sure you were all right before I started fiddling with the fuse-box. *Are* you all right, Dee-dee?"

"Yeah."

Bettina said, "But what's this?" She pulled the brandy bottle out of the wrought-iron loop.

Delia said, "Johnny put it there. I asked him to take it away, but he wouldn't."

Bettina sighed. She said, "Well, he's leaving in the morning." Holding torch and brandy bottle, she went indoors. Under the table, the insect-coil, burnt-out, stopped glowing.

A few minutes later, the lights came on: over the table, in Delia's room, in the hall.

Bettina came out of the house, smoking a cigarette. She went to the window. Delia was standing close to the guard. "All fixed," said Bettina.

"Shit! You have so many talents."

"Small talents."

"You're smoking. Your fifth. The last of the day."

"That's right."

"Shit, if I—" Delia didn't finish the sentence.

Bettina said, "It's a matter of discipline. Habit." Then, "I can't think where Johnny is. The door of his room's open, and he's not there."

"He was on the terrace for a bit, when he put the brandy here," Delia said. Then, "I thought I heard him going towards the steps. Perhaps he has gone for a walk."

Bettina said, "It seems an odd time to choose. With a big storm about to break. I'll just have a look."

She went towards the rail. She was wearing little white slippers. Something crunched under one of them. She frowned, and stooped. The cigarette dropped from her hand. She looked towards the table, then down at the paving. From her mouth came a long wavering howl.

Delia shouted, "*Bettina*!" But Bettina stood in silence. Then, "*Bettina*! What is it?"

Bettina called out—her voice trembled—"My cup! The maenad cup!"

"What's happened to it?"

"I forgot to take it in last night. I was so tired. I left it in the middle of the table, and now it's in fragments at the edge of the terrace."

"Oh, no. No!" Then, "Oh, shit—can't it be mended?"

"*No*!" But, after a moment, Bettina knelt down on the floor. Her hands moved among the shards, chips, dust of pottery. Then she found one fragment larger than the rest. Holding it, she laboured to her feet. She went over to the table where the lamp revealed, under the curve of an arm, a bowed rapt face.

Bettina kissed it. She placed the piece of pottery in the centre of the table where the cup had been. She stood upright, straightening her shoulders. But then—as a great flare lit the hillside, the house, the terrace, the three rocks in the turbulent sea, where a glint of fierce pink vanished for ever—Bettina ran to the rail. She raised her arms, as if pleading, to the sky; but the lightning did not strike her.

There was darkness. A crash of thunder made Bettina flinch. She lowered her arms to her sides. And then —agglomerate spears from a chariot in the sky—the rain descended. Bettina raised her face. She raised her hands to unknot her hair. Now, in fall of rain, in fall of hair, she was contained. Eyes closed, lips closed, she smiled.